MY FATAL VALENTINE
JUNIPER HOLIDAY BOOK 5

LEIGHANN DOBBS

CHAPTER ONE

"So there you have it, folks! Adrien Stewart! This is this year's Holiday Valentine's Day Exchange and Raffle Hottie King of Hearts!" Juniper held up Adrien's hand with one of her own. With the other, she egged the crowd on into offering hoots, hollers, catcalls, and whistles while Adrien grinned at all the attention he gathered from a veritable sea of Crescent Cove female eligibles.

Juniper couldn't blame the female Covians for hooting. Adrien was quite handsome, with velvety brown eyes, a square jaw, and arms like a lumberjack's. He didn't smell too bad, either, like a cross between dark, spiced cinnamon and the ocean. A scent which one lucky female would be savoring on their date later in the evening.

It was the Juniper Holiday annual Valentine's Day raffle, a charity event she put on every year. So far, everything about her Valentine's Day party had gone off without a hitch... unlike previous parties that had ended in murder.

But this one, held in the ballroom of her mansion, was going quite well, Juniper thought as she glanced around the room at the pink and red streamers and the heart and Cupid decorations. The tables were draped in white linen with a pattern of little hearts, and each had a centerpiece of red roses. The guests all looked happy as they eagerly anticipated the drawing for the lucky lady who would be Adrien's date.

After a moment, Juniper released Adrien's hand. "And now, ladies... let's get to the moment you've all been waiting for!"

Victoria Cooper, Juniper's goddaughter, pressed a button, and a digitized drumroll poured from the speakers placed strategically around the ballroom while Juniper herself turned the crank on an old bingo roller, inside of which was the name of every eligible female in the room, printed on little slips of folded paper.

Each person had paid a premium to be in the raffle, and there would be three winners of lesser prizes, with the grand prize being an all-expense-paid date with Adrien.

The drums stopped, and all the ladies waited with bated breath while Juniper reached in to pull out one of the slips of paper. She grinned. "Are you ready?"

The crowd of ladies all yelled together, "Yes!"

Juniper chuckled at their eagerness. "Very well, here we go. Our third runner-up—Miss Delilah Fontaine!"

Delilah, a cute little brunette wearing low-cut hot-pink silk bell bottoms and a short white shirt that showed off the belly-button ring in her navel, hopped up and down with excitement then turned to her left to hug her friend.

"Delilah, you win a five-hundred-dollar gift certificate to Just Jewels!" Just Jewels was a popular jewelry store in Crescent Cove.

Once the cheers faded and everyone got quiet again, Juniper nodded to Victoria. Drums again, then silence, then…

"Our second runner-up is… Miss Tracy Muller! Tracy wins a five-pound box of premium chocolates from Decadent Delights, and don't throw out those gold hearts—they're twenty-four carat!" Juniper had the premium chocolate store in town design special chocolates with little genuine gold hearts on some of them. "Yay, Tracy! Woot! You go, girl! Come on, everyone, give her a hand."

The crowd erupted in clapping, and Juniper grinned. Tracy Muller was a little more than a tad on the shy side. Her face was already three shades brighter red than it had been a moment before, and her eyes were wide despite telltale signs of excitement. Juniper figured she'd already started to sweat at the thought of winning a date with hunky Adrien Stewart, but hey, at least she was still smiling. Truth be told, Juniper had been hoping Tracy would win the date; she didn't hang with the popular crowd and rarely dated. It would have been nice for her.

Nodding for Tori to hit the drums again,

Juniper waited for the dramatic stretch of silence. "Okay, girls, this is the last runner-up before we pull the grand prize winner!" Juniper reached into the drum and pulled out a paper. "Miss Clarice Bellmont! You win gift certificates to Crescent Cove's finest restaurants—RarelyDone Steakhouse, Dusty Buns Bakery, and the Rotgut and Ruin local bar."

A whole section of ladies hooted and hollered in support of Miss Bellmont. Juniper didn't say a word, but she definitely knew why. Those snobbies, the little socialite "daddy-bought-me-a-BMW" girls, expected Clarice to win because, well, she was Crescent Cove's new mayor's daughter. The old mayor, Floyd Berkshaw, had been shot and killed by his wife, and the vice mayor had served for only three weeks before quitting and necessitating a quick election, which was won by Clarice's father, Johnny Bellmont.

Despite winning the best runner-up prize, Clarice didn't look happy. She'd probably been expecting to win the grand prize. Juniper was glad she hadn't. Clarice, along with her friends, Emma Porter, Lacey Hines, and Tiffany Davenport, had always been entitled. They were a few years younger than Tori, but Juniper remembered Tori telling her how they'd been rich mean girls in high school. Even though they were almost thirty now, Juniper could tell not much had changed.

Secretly, Juniper wouldn't have been surprised if the entitled ladies had tried to sneak in and rig the final roll, but she'd seen to it that they couldn't. Not only had she put the rollers under strict lock and key, she'd had Jacobi haunt the room where they were being kept—as a wholly cautious, totally preventative measure.

Tori had pressed another button on the machine, as per Juniper's prior direction, and a short interlude of music played while the runners-up took a moment or two to celebrate their positions before they pulled the big prize winner.

Silence fell, and right on cue, Tori started the drumroll up again. Juniper gave the crank a couple hearty spins and then clapped while it settled to a stop on its own before she stuck her hand in to choose this year's Queen of Hearts, the sweet little all-expenses-paid-by-

Juniper date with smokin'-hot Adrien Stewart winner.

"Ladies! And the winner is..."

Lover of drama that she was, Juniper waited, drawing the moment out as long as she possibly could before slowly unfolding the paper in her hand. "Oh, would you look at that? Miss Tiffany Davenport!"

She hurried to the edge of the makeshift stage she and Tori had put together a week ago. "Come on up here, Tiffany!"

Reaching back for Adrien's hand, she paused to give the newly chosen queen time to join them. Once she had, Juniper put Tiffany's hand in Adrien's and handed her a dozen long-stemmed red roses that were all neatly tied with a bow, and a box of chocolates.

Then, she motioned for Fedora Layhee, her neighbor and friend, to bring her the golden boxes.

Inside, each gold-wrapped box was lined with thick, cushiony velvet on which sat a glittering tiara and princely crown, respectively.

Juniper reached in and placed the jeweled pieces on this year's winners' heads while Fedora cheerfully slipped the sashes, which spelled out precisely who these two lovely people were, over their heads.

Juniper led the couple to the center of the stage. "Ladies! Gentlemen! Gather around, please! Today, I give to you the Juniper Holiday Valentine's Day Exchange and Raffle's own King and Queen of Hearts!"

Juniper plastered a smile on her face and looked out over the crowd. Truth be told, she had hoped one of the less prominent young ladies would have won. The crowd was clapping, and the mean-girl clique was hopping up and down—everyone except for Clarice, that is. Clarice was giving Tiffany a narrow-eyed gaze that did not look very friendly.

The rest of the crowd started back to their tables. Food would be served, and people would mill about, secretly leaving valentines at the place settings of the other guests. Juniper smiled over at Tori, hopeful that this was one party that would not have any type of incident that required the police.

CHAPTER TWO

"Juni," Fedora trilled. "The limo is here. Where are the king and queen? Everyone's ready to see them off."

"Everyone?" Juniper asked, pointedly looking around the still-crowded ballroom.

Fedora flapped her hand about. "You know what I mean."

"Yes, but do you? I mean, the definition of 'everyone' means everyone, Dora, dear. There are quite a few people still mingling here. Besides, it's not like they're getting married. It's just a date."

"Juniper Holiday, I'm quite tired of your

literalisms, thank you very much," Fedora said with a little huff.

Juniper chuckled. "I'm sorry, Dora. Sometimes, it's too easy to rile you people. I'll dial it back a bit, I suppose."

Fedora sniffed and gave a nod. "Thank you. Now," she said, scanning the crowd, "where is the Queen of Hearts?"

"I saw her hanging out near the chocolate fountain with a couple of ladies earlier," Tori said as she came over, having heard Fedora's question. "But I don't know where she's gone now."

Fedora frowned. "She knew the limo would be arriving at five o'clock, didn't she?"

"Yes," Juniper answered, nodding. "I made sure to let both her and Adrien know so they wouldn't wander off too far. Hunting people down in this place is a scavenger hunt in itself—ooh, there's an idea for Easter's activity, Tor! A scavenger hunt! Grand prize—a cool ten K."

"Let's not get ahead of ourselves, June," Tori said, searching the room for a sign of Tiffany. "Valentine's Day isn't over yet."

Her scan of the crowd revealed no signs of

Tiffany Davenport, and Tori frowned. "Where could she have gone?"

"Maybe she and Adrien slipped off together," Juniper suggested, her tone heavy with another implication.

Tori shook her head. "No, I don't think they would. At least, not for reasons you think, Juni. Adrien is kind of in a relationship with someone."

Juni gasped. "And I crowned him King of Hearts? This contest was open only to single, unattached people! Oooh, just wait till I find him! I'm going to give him a piece of my mind!"

"Brienne told him to enter," Tori explained. "She gave her full blessing. Said it was for a good cause."

Juniper frowned at her goddaughter. The raffle had an entry fee, with the proceeds going to the Crescent Cove Children's Hospital. "Well, I suppose the children's hospital is a good cause, and if Bree doesn't mind, then I guess it's okay. How do you know all this?"

Tori gave her a look. "I do live in the Cove, Juni. I know people just like you do."

Juniper sniffed. "I know that. My surprise

is warranted, though, considering how often you don't leave your room."

Tori arched her brow at the unspoken implication in Juniper's tone. "Do you want me to stop writing those stories you love?"

Juniper gasped. "You wouldn't!"

"Of course I wouldn't," Tori said. "But the time spent in my room is necessary."

"I know that. It just surprises me how much you know about people given how little you leave your room."

Tori cut a look at Juniper from the corner of her eye. "Mm-hmm."

"Ahem."

Tori and Juniper looked to Fedora, who was standing on Juniper's other side, looking like she was about to be in need of smelling salts.

Fedora blinked rapidly. "If you two are quite finished, I think we should go look for our missing queen. I'm sure Adrien is wondering where she is as well."

"Okay, but low-key," Juniper said. "I don't want everyone snooping around the place."

Tori rolled her eyes. "As if most of them haven't already."

"You want to win that point, Tortellini, but I'm not going to give it to you because it's too easy. Try harder, and you might get double points instead. Now, you and Dora go right. I'll go left and consult with the ghosts since they see stuff we miss. We'll meet back here in five, hopefully with our missing queen in tow. Okay? Okay. See you both in five."

Tori watched her godmother leave in a rush of gold and black sequins and shook her head. To Dora, she said, "We should get going. If I know her, she's counting down the seconds and will absolutely proclaim herself the winner if she gets back here before we do, whether she finds Tiffany or not."

Fedora gave a little sigh. "I know, dear. I know."

So without further ado, Tori and Fedora began their search for the missing Queen of Hearts. They searched the music room and the game room, the only empty room in the house, and the sunroom and the entertainment room, which was different from the game room in that it was the only room in which one could watch television, albeit on a gigantic theater screen.

None of the rooms led to Tiffany, and Tori knew it was time to check the bathrooms. The first one was empty, but the door of the second one had been left open a crack.

Approaching, Tori knocked and called out Tiffany's name but got no answer. Through the crack in the door, Tori could see something on the floor.

Tori pushed the door open a tiny bit more. "Tiffany? Are you in here? The limo's waiting outside, hon. Tiffany?"

Still no answer.

Frowning, Tori pushed the door open a couple inches more, and her eyes went wide. "Oh, no," she breathed.

"What is it?" Fedora asked, standing on her tiptoes to look over Tori's head into the bathroom. "What do you see?"

"Well, I'm not sure yet, Dora, but I think our Queen of Hearts might need medical assistance."

Fedora gasped. "Is she… she's not… I hope it's not another…"

"Maybe she just passed out from the excitement," Tori said hopefully as she went to the unconscious Tiffany lying on the bathroom floor and knelt next to her. She put her hand on her shoulder and gave a little shake. "Tiffany? Honey? You okay?"

Tiffany didn't move.

Tori's brows knit in a worried frown. She wasn't sure if she should try to turn her over… but she should probably move her hair out of in front of her face to check her breathing. As soon as she did so, she gasped and lurched back. Her heart sank, and her stomach twisted. Poor Tiffany…

To Fedora, she said, "Dora, go to the game room and call for an ambulance and the police. Tiffany Davenport is dead."

"Victoria Cooper, you did not just say what I think you said."

Turning to look over her shoulder, Tori found her godmother standing in the door, a mixed look of horror and anger on her face.

Tori pressed her lips together. "I don't think this Valentine's Day is going to be a very happy one, June."

CHAPTER THREE

"What is it with these people lately?" Juniper asked of no one as she stood in the space between the bathroom door and the body of this year's Queen of Hearts. Poor girl. Except for the banner proclaiming her as such, which had been tied extremely tight around her neck—Juniper assumed it was the girl's cause of death—she looked as if she might have fallen asleep right there on her side on the bathroom floor. "I can't even have a good party without someone going off all half-cocked and crazy. Bunch of lunatics. How do I keep inviting these kind of people?"

"They are not 'these kind of people,' June.

That's the sad bit," Tori said. "Whoever killed Tiffany is just a regular person like you and me. The only difference is that they've snapped into straight-up insanity for one reason or another."

Juniper's expression was frown heavy. "No. No, I refuse to be lumped into the melting pot with someone like whoever did this, Tor. These loons are not like us. Anyone who would kill another human being without extreme—and I do mean *extreme*—provocation is nothing like you and I."

"Detective Mallard should be here soon," Tori told her. "I'm sorry you have to deal with this again, June."

"It's starting to get to me, you know?" Juniper poked her head out of the bathroom door, scanning the now-crowded hallway for the familiar face of the Duckman. "Mr. Waddles should have been here ten minutes ago, Tori. Why don't you go find out what's taking so long?"

Tori gave her a look. "You sure you can hold back this crowd on your own?"

"Let one of them try to get past me." Juniper straightened. The fierceness of her emotions showing on her face, she said, "Just let them try."

"Lucky for us, Terrence and Fedora have already put the contestants into separate areas. The rest of the guests aren't going to be happy to have to wait for permission to leave, but..." Tori stepped between Juniper and the door. "You sure you'll be okay here while I go look for Desmond?"

Juniper nodded. "I'll be fine. I'll just look around to see if I can find anything that would help us figure out who did this to poor Tiffany."

As soon as the door closed behind Tori, Juniper's thoughts kicked into a more analytical gear. She scanned the door, the walls, the floor. There could be clues anywhere and everywhere. There should have been clues. But at the moment, she didn't really see anything beyond the "Queen of Hearts" ribbon around the neck of the deceased. It could be checked for fingerprints, couldn't it? So could the doorknob, the sink, the toilet, the mirror... all of which was probably as useless as trying to ask Tiffany herself who killed her.

Everyone in the mansion had been in this bathroom today at least once.

But wait, what was that smudge on the sash? Juniper looked closer at the brownish smudge. Dried blood was brownish, wasn't it? Tiffany didn't appear to have bled, though her throat had a nasty purple line where the sash had cut off her airflow. If the blood wasn't from her, maybe it was from the killer.

Jacobi floated into the room, his vaporous expression immediately sad. "Oh, dear. Another one."

"It's a pity one of you three can't talk to this girl. Ask her who did this," Juniper told him. "I can't move the body to look for clues that might be under her because the Duckster will have my head. Can you see anything, Jacobi?"

"Well, mum, I'd say the ribbon, but it is very obvious."

"Wait, something is off. Where in the world is her cell phone? Young ladies these days don't go anywhere without them. Where is Tiffany's?"

"I have no way of knowing, madam." Jacobi shrugged then suggested, "There is one thing you could try—if you wanted to see who killed the young miss."

"Anything, Jac."

Juniper's eyes must have reflected her near desperation because he did a surprised ghost blink kind of thing then cleared his throat for no reason. "Back in the day—er, my day, that is—some of us knew people who were different from others, if you take my meaning. A few of those folk were well versed in creating solutions."

"Finding Tiffany's killer before this whole 'another death at the Holiday mansion' thing gets into the ear of some of the local media and then out of hand would be a fine solution, Jacobi," Juniper said.

Jacobi held up a hand, ethereal though it was. "Not that type of solution, madam. I was referring to the art of mixing certain liquids and powders which could then be poured onto glass." He pointed at the mirror.

Her interest definitely snagged, Juniper rushed to the bathroom door and positioned her foot against it so it could not be opened from the outside unless she allowed it, then she turned to Jacobi and demanded, "Explain. Quickly."

"Alchemists, sorcerers, magicians—there were few in that time, but those who were especially skilled could whip up a solution which could capture the last image or reflection in a mirror or on glass at the time a soul passed on from this life…"

"You mean…" Juniper's eyes went wide. "I need to find Tori."

"Yes, madam. Would you like for me to stay here with the body, madam?"

Juniper started to refuse, since Jacobi was a ghost. Him staying was the equivalent of leaving the body without a witness to most of the living world. Then she remembered good old Duckbutt had had a crossover recently that allowed him to communicate with those who still lingered though they were physically dead. "Yes! Yes, Jacobi, you stay here and wait for Detective Mallard. And thank you so much for your suggestion. We may have this case wrapped up and closed before the chocolate-mousse hearts melt!"

Excited now as much as relieved, Juniper ran out of the bathroom and down the hallway, ignoring the urgent questions of those she passed in her rush. Jacobi had mentioned alchemy and potions and such, and she knew just who she needed to pay a visit. She only needed to collect her purse and keys first.

CHAPTER FOUR

With Queen's "Don't Stop Me Now" blaring through her speakers, Juniper pulled up in front of the WitchRoast Café. The place was semipacked with regulars and new lovers on coffee dates. Any other time, Juniper would think it cute and adorable seeing people out together, but today there just happened to be another murder at her home, and she didn't have the brain space to waste on such thoughts.

There were about four people waiting in line in front of her, and despite the voice in her head screaming at her to tell them to get the heck out of the way, that she had an emergency, she held her tongue and stood on her tiptoes instead, craning her neck to see if Quincy was working the counter today or if it was someone else.

Adeline noticed her and waved.

Juniper twisted the frown wanting to form into a smile and waved back. Beside her, she heard her name spoken.

"Fancy seeing you here," Quincy said. "I thought for sure you'd be at home for another couple of hours."

"Oh, thank God," she breathed, turning to him. "Quince, you gotta help me."

He frowned, concern etched on his face. "What's wrong?"

Juniper started to tell him, but noticing the curious gazes trained their way, she decided to go a more secluded route instead. "Uh, it's kind of…personal. Can we talk in your office?"

"Sure," Quincy said with a nod. "Follow me."

Juniper did gladly.

He called to Adeline and Holly that he'd be back in a few and to hold the place down until his return and then directed Juniper to follow him to the back.

Quincy's office was exactly how you'd expect it to be; ordered and labeled down to the pencil cup on his desk. It was fancy as all get-out, but everything had its place.

He went around the cherry-wood desk to sit in his very fine high-backed chair and motioned for Juniper to take a seat in one of the smaller chairs in front of it, which she did. Before he could ask again what was wrong, Juniper was talking.

Naturally, she got ahead of herself a time or two, and he had her start over.

Loosing a growl of frustration, she said, "Oh, for heaven's sake, Quince. Somebody died, and I need your help finding the killer!"

Quincy blinked. "And how do you presume I'm going to do that, June?"

Juniper tried not to chew her lip, but lord, it was difficult. "You're a witch, right? Or a warlock?"

"Witch works."

"Right. I have it on very good authority that witches, sorcerers, wizards, what have you —oh, Jac told me another word—what was it? Ah! Alchemists. Yes. Magic-y people can make a potion or something that will show the last moments of a dying person in a mirror when applied. Can you do that? It would make this whole murder-solving thing go way faster, let me tell you. And the less time I have to deal with the boys in blue, the better."

Quincy chuckled quietly at her explanation then leaned back in his chair and propped his elbows on the arms, steepling his fingers together. He regarded her closely for a moment then said, "I can work the magic necessary for such a thing, yes. But it will take time, Juniper, and materials I don't have readily at hand."

"Name it, and I bet I can get it."

He shook his head. "It's not that simple. They have to be purchased from someone brought up in the ways of my people. We alone are the ones who can pay the price required."

"Okay, fine. I can respect that. What about the time to make it? You need me to cover a shift or two?"

"No," he said, shaking his head again. "It must be worked under the light of the moon from first quarter to full. When it is complete, I alone must apply the potion to the surface of the mirror you wish to see the last moments in."

"That's absolutely doable. You know I've been trying to get you to my place for years, Quince," she said with a wink. "That it's under such horrible circumstances is not the best, but it is what it is, yeah?" She stood to leave. "Can I come pick it up, or do you have to deliver it to the house yourself?"

"Juniper, before you agree to this, you have to know that there is some risk involved in that it might not work. Calling forth such images is tricky because you can't be sure what the last thing reflected on the mirror's surface was. If you're okay with that, then I'll agree to work the spell. If not, I wish you the best in solving this crime."

Cocking her hip to the side and resting her hand on it, Juniper said, "Sweetie, if it keeps me from having to breathe the same air as Quackbutt for too long, I don't care what the risks are."

Quincy inclined his head in a nod, the slightest hint of a smile lurking at the corners of his mouth. "Then you have a deal."

*B*ack at the mansion, Tori was paying attention—as much as she could—while the ME examined and collected the body and the detectives covered the crime scene, which just happened to be the Holiday ballroom bathroom.

She was also busy shooing away the mansion cats, Ludo, Loki, and Finn. Loki had a penchant for sniffing people's shoes and was trying desperately to get at the shoes of the policemen. Ludo was strutting around showing off his fluffy tail. Finn was the biggest problem—the sleek gray cat had been seen chasing something down the hallways at night. Juniper was afraid it might be a mouse. Tori had had to stop him from running into the bathroom a few times as he streaked past, apparently chasing something.

A moment presented itself, and she waved to Detective Mallard.

"I was wondering if you'd found Miss Davenport's cell phone?"

"If a cell phone was collected, it will be

mentioned in the report, Miss Cooper," he told her.

Tori noticed something in the way his eyes hooded, the slight droop in the set of his usually straight shoulders, the tiniest drag in his normally sure-footed step that gave her pause. "What happened, Desmond?"

"A young woman was strangled with her lovely Queen of Hearts banner, Miss Cooper," he said, his tone of voice deadpan.

Tori wanted to snort at his choice to state the obvious. It was such a Juniper thing to do. Again, however, there was something in his eyes she didn't remember having seen before —something like... worry or maybe pain? Her brows drew together in a frown, and she moved toward him. Her hand went immediately to his brow to check for heat. "Are you all right, Detective Mallard?"

"We have everything, sir," Ackers said from his left. Desmond nodded.

"I will meet you back at the precinct in half an hour," he assured the man then waited in silence as his team departed the mansion. Intuition told Tori she should hold her tongue as well.

As soon as his team members were gone, Desmond turned to Tori, a hard look in his eyes. "Keep your godmother occupied, Miss Cooper. I'd greatly appreciate it if you make sure she doesn't get herself involved in this."

"Something happened at work?" Tori asked. She didn't know how she knew, but she had a feeling... one he confirmed with his next words.

"To put it simply, my job is on the line. If Juniper interferes again, it'll likely cost me my badge."

CHAPTER FIVE

By the time Juniper made it back to the mansion, all her partygoers were gone. Sent home by Detective Fanny-Feathers, no doubt. Tori told her there were a few suspects who had been asked to come to the precinct, but she didn't say who.

"You have to leave this one alone, June. Desmond is going to lose his job if you don't" was what she did say.

Juniper waved off her concern. "Don't worry your pretty little head, Torto. If my sources are as good as I think they are—and they are—we've got this one in the bag."

Tori was a bit taken aback. In the bag? How? Even the detective was scarce on leads.

"Sources? What are you talking about? What have you done now, Juniper Holiday?"

"I haven't done anything. Nor am I going to. Well, I am, but not in relation to this whole Valentine's Day debacle." Once again, she waved away Tori's fear. "We will find Tiffany's killer soon enough, believe me. Until then, now that this party has been sufficiently ruined, I need to get my I's dotted and my T's crossed for the Easter scavenger hunt."

"Who will come?" Fedora asked from the open door.

"Terrence let me in," she explained at Juniper's questioning look. Then she said, "Juniper, I think you might have a problem getting people to attend yet another party here. You now have a record of things going very badly."

Juniper's brows snapped together. "A problem? A record? What kind of ridiculous nonsense are you spouting now, Dori?"

"Well, while the detectives were busy assessing the crime scene and the rest of us were forced to hang out listening to low-level B-side music in the background, more than a few of your guests told me they are concerned over your parties now."

"Why would they be? I mean, it's not like I set out to have a murder occur, you know." In a huff now, Juniper rounded her desk and sat. "The fact is that the murderers in these cases were already looking to murder. A party makes a great cover since there are tons of suspects around. Maybe instead of concerning themselves with my parties, they should worry over their own behavior. Their own dark and sinister thoughts and their own lack of self-control."

Like with twenty-twenty vision, Tori had enough hindsight experience to know where this was going. "Fedora, I know what you're saying, but honestly, it's only one or two of the guests who are getting their drawers in a twist. Most of our attendees are oblivious to anything other than the great music, the wonderful food, and the fun to be had at a Juniper Holiday event."

Juniper smiled, and Tori knew she'd managed to mollify her. One down, one to go. She turned to pin Fedora with a look. "Only the guilty or suspected have been pulled aside, out of the festive atmosphere of the parties, really. Everyone else has been having the time of their lives, and you know it."

"It's true everyone loves a Holiday party. What's not to love about them when Juniper puts in so much time and effort?" Fedora nodded that she understood the hint in Victoria's eyes. Still, she put in one last warning. "I'm sure we don't need to worry about the few who chafe at the idea of receiving an invite now. The ones who are looking over their shoulders for no reason, wondering if your guest lists are secret hit lists. It's not *my* fault the top question on *those* people's minds is 'Who's next?'"

Tori closed her eyes, almost drowning in oh-my-word-why-didn't-she-just-leave-it-alone-and-let-me-handle-it regret. She should have stepped in, should have stopped Fedora the second she became aware that June's friend wasn't going to let this issue lie. So why hadn't she?

Her eyes popped open again at the sound of Juniper's laugh. "Chafe? What century are you living in, Dor? Nobody says 'chafe' anymore. Heck, *we* didn't even say 'chafe' when we were in the height of our phase of saying words that didn't make sense to most people."

"Sorry." Fedora's nose rose a half inch. "I've been reading again. You know how I get after I've consumed a few good books."

"Hmm, slipping into the language of the lost, that's how you get." Juniper's eyes cut quickly to Tori. "Hey, they should make a series off that. Language of the Lost."

She snapped her fingers then said, "Tor, do you remember that show that used to come on about a cave and Sleestaks and a sea monster?"

"Not really," Tori told her. "But I do remember Detective Mallard being most serious about you leaving this case alone, Juniper. He is worried he will lose his job, which means I'm worried you won't be worried about it. Are you?"

Juniper gave her a curious look. She had Quincy and his spell casting on the job. She would wait the given time and let him do what he did. Did she want to tell Tori-bori what she'd done? Yes. Was she going to? No. Why? Because sometimes, Tori was a party pooper, and Juniper didn't need that or her logic right now.

That said, she wasn't going to leave her completely in the dark. She was mischievous sometimes and devious a lot of times, but cruel? Never.

"Am I worried? Not one bit. Got it covered, remember? Now. Fedora." She straightened, cracked her knuckles, and spun her desk chair so she could look out the window. "What do you think about filling that pool out there with Jell-O?"

CHAPTER SIX

*D*esmond sat at his desk, his gaze unfocused, contemplative. Tiffany Davenport's file lay open in front of him. He hadn't looked at it in... minutes... hours... days? Who knew? It felt like weeks. Then again, it was possible he was suffering from the effects of having to work another homicide in only a few weeks' time. It was starting to wear on him. He didn't know what it was about Juniper Holiday or her mansion, but there had to be an explanation as to why people kept dying on the premises. Granted, Hannah Peterson's death had occurred in the mortuary, but her body had ended up on Holiday property.

Maybe the place was cursed?

He snorted as soon as the thought entered his mind. He was not one given to fanciful explanations. He thought them more excuses than anything.

But you can see ghosts now, a voice reminded him in the recesses of his mind. He glared at nothing and responded with "No one asked you."

"What's that, Boss?" Harvey Nichols asked, sticking his head in the doorway of Desmond's office.

"Nothing," he said, waving the man away. "I was just talking to myself."

"You know," Harvey began, slinking further inside the room, "they say talking to yourself is one of the first signs of insanity. You ain't losing your marbles, are you, Boss?"

Desmond's stare could have turned Medusa to stone. On Harvey, it had no effect. Desmond's nostrils flared. "No. I am not 'losing my marbles,' Nichols. Did you get the report from that smudge on the sash?"

"Yes, sir. That's why I was coming by. Turns out it was chocolate."

Desmond nodded. He'd thought as much.

"Can they analyze the ingredients? Perhaps narrow it down to where the chocolate came from?"

"They're on it." Nichols said. "I was just on my way out when I heard you talking to yourself, and I thought I'd stop by and see if you needed me to do anything else before I headed out."

Desmond was already shaking his head before Nichols had finished speaking. "No. You may leave, Nichols."

Harvey ducked his head in a quick nod, grinning like he'd won some grand prize rather than just going home for the night. "Goodnight, sir! I'll say a prayer for you tonight, sir, that you get this case solved real quick like."

"Thank you, Nichols," Desmond said sincerely. He had a feeling he was going to need all the help he could get, especially since he had to be on his toes about making sure Juniper didn't try to weasel her way into solving the murder. Again. His boss had been very unhappy that Juniper had ended up at the confession scene of the last murder again, and Desmond needed to solve this one without her trying to beat him to the punch. There was too much riding on him doing his job.

Harvey nodded again and turned to leave, but then, for some reason Desmond could not fathom—and barely tolerated—he turned back around, a concerned frown on his face. "You know, sir, I can't help but think this is all so strange."

With a sigh that he forced to be quiet, Desmond leaned back in his chair, mentally preparing himself for a long few minutes of idle chatter. "You can't help but think what is strange?"

"All these murders and things that keep happenin' to Ms. Holiday. Why, if I didn't know any better, I'd say somebody's tryin' to set her up, you know? Either that, or that place of hers is haunted."

Desmond bit back the knee-jerk response that ghosts weren't real. He'd been witness to the reality of the paranormal too many times now to deny their existence any longer. But he wasn't about to affirm what everyone speculated about the Holiday mansion. It was indeed haunted, but the spirits residing there were hardly the malevolent type. Sarcastic? Yes. Stuffy? Absolutely. But cruel? Definitely not. No, the only cantankerous soul in residence there was none other than Juniper Holiday herself.

Suddenly, Desmond realized with a start that Harvey was still talking. He'd zoned out some time ago. He only hoped he'd nodded and made the appropriate noises of agreement as Harvey prattled on. Seeing that he wasn't staring at him like he'd truly lost his mind, he must have done something right.

"Anyway, goodnight, sir. Don't stay here too long. I'm sure your bed misses you," Harvey said with a wink as he finally left.

For long minutes after his exit, Desmond sat pondering his words. Perhaps the Holiday mansion was haunted by something other than the spirits of servants long gone from this plane. Perhaps he could ask them if they knew something... He shook his head as soon as the thought entered his mind.

Perhaps he really was losing his mind. Why else would he entertain the thought of stepping foot inside that place, knowing he risked the chance of running into Juniper?

You could always ask a favor of Miss Cooper, that voice whispered in his head again. This time, he didn't immediately dismiss it as he began spinning a plan. He could ask Victoria to make sure her godmother was occupied elsewhere for a few hours while he talked to the ghosts. He glanced at the clock, noting the late hour, and disappointment filled him. It was far too late to ring her. Tomorrow morning, he decided.

Nodding to himself, he began gathering his things, pausing for a moment before turning off the desk lamp to stare at the picture of Tiffany Davenport one more time. In this picture, she was smiling brightly, her eyes filled with all the wonder of living. He preferred to remember the victims of the cases he worked as happy, though it wasn't always possible.

"You shall have justice, Miss Davenport. I promise," he said to her picture. Then he closed the file, slipped it into his briefcase, turned off the lamp, and left his office, locking the door behind him.

The lightest scent of lavender filled his nostrils as he made his way out of the building, giving him pause. Standing next to his car, he looked around, scanning the shadows for a sign that someone was there. Finding none, he chalked it up to a lack of sleep and got in his car after unlocking the door.

Ghosts didn't have a reflection, which was why he didn't see Tiffany standing next to the car in his side mirror, a soft smile on her face.

He drove off, and she faded away.

CHAPTER SEVEN

Tori wasn't quite sure how it happened, but she was standing in Juniper's office with Detective Mallard while he interviewed "the ghosts" and keeping watch on the door in case her godmother decided to come back as he did so.

"I still don't understand why you feel you need to sneak around to do this, Desmond," she told him. "June says the ghosts are loyal to her. That means the minute you're gone, they will flock to her to let her know what you are up to."

"By the time she's informed, I will be gone, so it will hardly matter, Miss Cooper.

Now, where is the other one—Jack or something like that?" Desmond asked.

"She cannot see us, sir," Felicity reminded him. "There is no way she could know only two of us answered your summons."

Tori saw Desmond wince and wondered at the cause. He did not elaborate. Instead, he asked, "Could one of you please ask Mr. Jacobi to join us?"

"Absolutely not, Mr. Mallard," Lionel told him. "And his name is merely Jacobi for the time being, the same as I am Lionel, and she is Felicity. Nothing more, nothing less."

Desmond sighed. "Very well. Let's get on with it. You both must know I am working the case involving the death of Miss Tiffany Davenport. Since you three... um... hang out here? Yes, since you're here, I was hoping one of you had seen something. Anything, really. Did you?"

Tori busied herself with only listening to the one-sided conversation. Not only could she not see Juniper's ghosts, she could not hear them, either.

"Unfortunately, we were all busy elsewhere, sir," Lionel said. "Although…" The ghost turned to Felicity. "Lissy was patrolling the shadows and corners." He returned his attention to Desmond. "You know how foolish the young can be, I presume."

After a moment of silence during which he perused Desmond from head to toe and back again, he said, "Or perhaps not."

"Yes, yes, I understand what you're saying," Desmond told him. He ignored the slight flush creeping from beneath his collar. "Young people sometimes prefer the solitude of a darkened corner. Was Tiffany one of them?"

"Not at all," Lionel told him. "She seemed more interested in enjoying her moment with the rest of her peers."

"She did have a more private word with that Hines girl," Felicity offered. "It was almost time for the limo to arrive. Miss Davenport waved her over, and I was intrigued, so I floated over as well. Of course, neither of the girls saw me…"

"What happened?" Desmond broke in. "What did they discuss?"

Felicity cocked her head to the side, and one of her ghostly curls spilled from her bonnet. A wistful smile crossed her lips, and she shook her head. "I'm sure it's nothing pertinent, Detective Mallard. Just a girl thing, really."

"Please. Let me decide what is and is not pertinent," Desmond told her, his tone a bit forceful, which drew Tori's attention.

"Um, maybe don't get gruff with this lot, Detective?" she suggested. "If what June says is true, this lot will go silent as a grave, mum as a mummy, quiet as a tomb if they feel pressured."

Felicity chuckled at Tori's warning, though Desmond was the only living soul who could hear it. "She's right, Detective Mallard. You wouldn't want to risk that, would you?"

Desmond's sigh was long and filled with resignation. "Of course not, Miss—ah, Felicity. All I want to do is figure out who took the life of a brilliant young woman with a bright future ahead of her. If you—or either of you—can help me with that, I would certainly appreciate it."

Felicity exchanged a look with Lionel. He

nodded, and she turned back to the detective. "Miss Davenport called Miss Hines aside and asked the girl if she'd help protect the evening for her by taking some pictures of her leaving for the date and then holding her cell phone until it was over. She did not want anything distracting from the lovely arrangement Ms. Holiday had created for her. She knew it wasn't a real encounter with the gentleman of the evening, of course, but she wanted to enjoy every moment just the same."

Desmond's eyes went wide, and Tori's brow lowered. "What is it? Is it bad?"

He held up a hand, silencing Tori's questions. To Felicity, he said, "She gave Miss Hines her phone? You're certain?"

"Absolutely." Felicity nodded. "I watched Miss Hines tuck it away in her purse myself."

"Who? Who gave Lacey Hines a phone?" Tori asked, but Desmond didn't answer.

There was something else scratching at the back of his thoughts, another question he needed to ask before he left the Holiday house. "Why did Jack decline to meet with me?"

"You mean Jacobi, sir, and that is his business, I suppose," Lionel answered.

"Hmph," Desmond retorted in response. "It sure looks as if Mr. Jack has something to hide."

"He just didn't want to tell you he'd pointed me to a surefire method to find out who killed Tiffany Davenport is all," Juniper said from the doorway.

Desmond jumped, and the ghosts didn't bother to try to hide their smiles. "Ms. Holiday. I thought you were out on an errand."

"So that's why you decided to sneak into my house, interrogate my innocent ghosties? Because you thought I would not be here? If you wanted a private word with my ghosts, WaddlePants, it could have been arranged without all the subterfuge and without dragging my goddaughter into it. Why not ask me, Duckman?"

Juniper gave him a look and pretended to be wounded, but he doubted she felt the least bit hurt by his obvious exclusion of her from the—uh—interrogation. What he did see, however, was that she truly was piqued that Tori would let him in without her being present, and coming between Juniper Holiday and her much-loved goddaughter was the last thing he wanted. "Don't blame Tori, Ms. Holiday. It was my idea. I—I needed to speak with them alone, without you standing guard."

Juniper's laugh was almost a cackle. "You thought my absence would make a difference, Captain Waddles?"

Hesitant, he nodded, and she laughed again.

"Well, you are wrong. My friends are loyal, regardless of my presence. I'm sure they wouldn't tell you anything I wouldn't have told you myself had I known."

"Did you know Tiffany gave Lacey Hines her cell phone?" Tori asked.

"I did not. But I really don't need to. I have other ways of learning things, of knowing what happened, Victoria. As for you." She turned to the detective. "I assume you don't have any good leads if you are here trying to get clues from the ghosts. How about that smudge on the sash. It could have been blood from the killer."

Desmond shook his head. Did Juniper actually think he hadn't noticed the smudge or had it analyzed? "Not blood. Chocolate."

"Darn. But I guess that would have been

too easy. But now I guess you have a new clue thanks to Felicity and Lionel. Shouldn't you be hightailing it over to the Hines girl's place? Better hurry before she tries to ditch that cell, hmm?"

CHAPTER EIGHT

"You're never going to be nice to him, are you?"

Juniper blinked owlishly at Tori's question, her hand going to her chest in a sign of affront, fingers splayed wide. "You think I was being mean?"

Tori rolled her eyes and pushed away from the wall she'd been leaning against. "You definitely weren't being nice."

"I was helping him, believe it or not, Tor."

A mirthless laugh fell from Tori's lips. "How was any of *that* helpful, Juni? He's only trying to do his job, you know, and part of that is asking questions. He thought your ghosts might know something and was probably correct in assuming you would laugh him off the property if he asked you if he could talk to them."

Juniper crossed her arms and regarded Tori quietly for a moment, her gaze scrutinizing. "You really think that little of me, kiddo?"

"Juniper, you know I think very highly of you," Tori said, shaking her head, "but you can come across as a—"

"Don't say it," Juniper said, holding her hand up.

Tori sighed. "I wasn't gonna use that word, thank you very much."

Juniper's brow went up.

"I was going to say *harridan*, but you have a habit of jumping to conclusions."

"Psh. I do not."

Tori cocked her head to the side, both brows raised.

"All right, maybe sometimes, I can fly off the handle," Juniper said, flicking her fingers dismissively. "It's hardly often enough to call me a harridan."

Tori scoffed, a smile flitting across her lips.

Juniper's demeanor softened, and she

moved closer to Tori, hugging her. "I'm sorry I'm being mean to your Duckman."

"He's not my—"

"Save it. He might not have asked yet, but anyone with eyes can see he fancies you." She leaned close to stage-whisper, "I think he's scared of me."

"I don't think he is," Tori said, shaking her head.

Juniper put her finger on Tori's lips to silence her. "It's a healthy fear, dear. And I really was helping him earlier."

Tori's features squished in a frown. "How?"

Juniper grinned. "I told him about the cell phone and who had it."

"You did not. One of the ghosts did. Speaking of, are they still here?" Tori asked, looking around the empty room.

"Just who do you think gave them the idea to let that little tidbit slip, dearest? And yes, they are. They're just being quiet right now."

Tori hummed then shook her head and said, "Wait, you knew about the cell phone?"

"Not before Lissy did, but I did tell her to let Sir Feathers know about it if he showed up, since, you know, I'm not supposed to be getting involved in this case. I know his boss came down hard on him when I solved the mayor's murder, and I'm trying to give him a fair chance."

Tori folded her arms and gave Juniper a scrutinizing look. "I don't know if I believe you. It's a little too convenient, even for you."

Juniper shrugged. "Your belief or disbelief of the matter doesn't make the truth any less true. Now, stop being mad at me for playing my little game with the Duckster, please. There's an unspoken agreement between us that allows us to coexist only so long as we don't get chummy."

Tori didn't look like she bought into that, but the conversation was cut short by Finn streaking past them in the hallway.

"Oh no, he's chasing something again," Tori said. "Maybe we should call someone. I think we have mice."

"Call someone? Like an exterminator?" Juniper felt squeamish. She hated the idea of harming an animal, even if it was a mouse. "That sounds harsh. Can't we just coexist with the mice sort of like I'm doing with the Duckman?"

♥

Across town, Desmond fought back a sneeze. After the initial burn and subsequent watering of the eyes dissipated, he got out of his parked sedan and walked up the stone path to the front door of 867 Crescent View Lane and knocked three times.

A moment later, he noticed the curtain at the window near the door flutter as someone peeked out, then the door opened and Lacey Hines stood before him with a not-so-confident smile on her face.

"Detective Mallard," she greeted. "What brings you by?"

Desmond nearly choked, as the first words that came to mind were entirely unprofessional and only something he could imagine Juniper voicing at such an inopportune time. Clearing his throat to regain his composure and control of the situation, he explained about Tiffany Davenport.

Lacey's face fell at the first mention of

Tiffany's name. "I already know about her death, Detective. It absolutely broke my heart to hear about it. She was so young, you know. It's one of those things you can't imagine happening to you or someone you know, and yet it has, and I—"

Her words ended abruptly on a sob, and she buried her face in her hands.

Desmond reached into his jacket pocket and retrieved a handkerchief he kept on hand for moments such as this.

Lacey accepted the handkerchief and apologized for her sudden tears.

"There's no need for an apology, Miss Hines. A tragic thing has happened. Did you know Miss Davenport personally?"

Sniffling, Lacey nodded as she dabbed at her eyes. "Tiffany and I were friends. She was always so happy and outgoing." She sniffled again and looked at Desmond inquiringly. "Do you have any idea who would have done such a thing?"

"That's what I wanted to talk to you about, Miss Hines. Was Miss Davenport acting strange at all when she gave you her phone? Did it seem like she wanted it safe and out of harm's way?"

Lacey shook her head. "Not any more than anyone wouldn't want their phone getting messed up. She didn't want to keep getting interrupted by calls and pings, so she asked if I would keep it until the date was over. She was nervous."

Desmond nodded as he filed away that information for later. "Do you know anyone who would have wanted to harm her?"

"No, that's the thing. Everyone loved her." Lacey glanced down the street and twisted the heart bracelet on her wrist nervously. "I hope there isn't a random killer on the loose."

"I don't think you need to worry. It appears this killing was personal."

Lacey gasped. "You mean she knew her killer? Oh dear. Poor Tiffany. If there's anything I can do to help…"

"You can, actually. That's why I'm here. Could I have Tiffany's phone?"

Lacey frowned up at him, shaking her head slightly. "I don't have it, Detective. I dropped it off this morning. One of your men said they would take care of it."

Desmond felt his expression smooth out. "Can you tell me who you gave it to?"

"Um… I can't remember his name, exactly," Lacey said, running her fingers through her hair. "He had a real welcoming face, though."

"Nichols."

"Yes! That's him! I gave it to Detective Nichols."

Desmond sighed internally and nodded to Lacey. "Thank you for your time, Miss Hines. Sorry for bothering you."

"It's not a bother, Detective," she said. "I just hope it helps y'all find Tiffany's killer. She didn't deserve it."

Desmond made his goodbyes and went back to his car, plotting all sorts of torture for Harvey when he saw him next for his failure to tell him they already had the cell phone in their possession.

CHAPTER NINE

When Desmond arrived at the precinct, Adrien Stewart's girlfriend, Brienne Porter, was waiting for him in a conference room. He'd asked for her to be brought in for questioning despite Victoria's having told him Adrien had had her full approval for the Valentine's Day date that was to be Juniper's prize. The fact was, she could have just said that she approved to make herself look good… or innocent. First, however…

"Nichols! My office. Now. Wait for me," he said then walked into the conference room to speak with Miss Brienne Porter about her boyfriend and Tiffany Davenport.

"Good afternoon, Detective." She greeted him with an open, friendly smile. "I assume I'm here to talk to you about Tiffany?"

Desmond nodded. "Among other things. How's Adrien, Miss Porter? Are you and he having trouble?"

Confusion clouded her eyes. "No, we aren't. In fact, he dropped me off here just a little while ago. Is something wrong?"

Desmond sat across the table from her, flipped open a file, and put a picture of Tiffany on the table where she could see it. "Nothing other than the fact that this girl is dead. Tell me, Miss Porter, why would Adrien accept the role of King of Hearts, knowing it involved going on a date... and why would you let him?"

Her gaze flew up to lock with his, surprise and maybe a little bit of fear in her eyes. "What do you mean? It was just a date for charity. Why wouldn't I agree to that?"

"Let's just say I find it very odd that a guy in a perfectly happy relationship would join a Valentine's date raffle and also odd that his girlfriend wouldn't be jealous."

Brienne's surprise and fear turned to

something like offense. Desmond could feel the vibes rolling off her, and every one of them said he'd managed to insult her. "Look, Detective, maybe you're not the kind of guy who can understand when people want to do a good deed, but I'm telling you that is exactly what Adrien and I had in mind. We talked about the date raffle. We already know every eligible woman in the Cove would love to spend an evening with him—he's handsome, witty, fun... every girl's dream. Especially mine."

"So why would you jeopardize your dream? Why allow for the possibility of it becoming a nightmare by suggesting he enter the raffle and spend a romantic evening with someone else?"

"That one should be obvious, Detective Mallard. I can already have a date with Adrien whenever I want."

"It just seems like inviting trouble, Miss Porter, and I don't see why any normal, happily together couple would invite trouble into their relationship."

"There would have been no trouble if Tiffany hadn't died. We wanted there to be a lot of entries because the children's hospital charity is one that's close to my heart." Brienne looked up at him, her eyes moist. "My baby sister had cancer when she was seven, and the hospital helped her immensely."

Desmond was taken aback. "Oh, I'm sorry."

Brienne shrugged. "She's okay now. But you can see why I didn't mind lending Adrienne out for the night if it meant more money would be raised. Adrien and I have a solid relationship. We are happy. The date wasn't meant to be a forever thing with whoever won, and nobody should have died because of it."

Because of it. For some reason, those words gave Desmond pause. Was the fact Tiffany won the date the motive for murder, or was it something else? Maybe he was currently barking up the wrong tree? He put the picture back, closed the folder, and stood. "Thank you for your time, Miss Porter."

Brienne nodded. "I was happy to come down and answer your questions, Detective. Tiffany's death has upset us all. If there is anything else I can help with, let me know. We all want to know who would have done this to her."

Desmond waited while she collected her purse and then made her way out of the precinct before making his own way to his office, where Harvey Nichols waited. As always, Harvey was smiling when he slammed open the door.

"Tiffany's cell phone—you have it?" Desmond demanded.

Still smiling, Harvey nodded several times as he answered. "Yes, sir, Detective, sir. Had it since this morning. It's been down at forensics for hours. I guess they should have something to tell us soon, sir. Want me to call you when they do?"

"What I would have preferred would have been a call from you the minute Miss Hines brought the phone in. Why didn't that happen, Harvey?"

He shrugged. "I figured you'd know about it, sir, since you were going to have a chat with the lady yourself. She didn't tell you? She should have told you."

"*You* should have told me, Harvey. You. Now there's no telling how long I'll have to wait before forensics gets back with…" He stopped, closed his eyes, and started counting. After a minute, he opened his eyes. "Never mind, Nichols. I'll get the information when I get it."

♥

♥

Across town, Juniper asked Quincy the question that had been bugging her since he'd let her know his people had the ingredients needed to make her mirror potion. He'd just slid her a double-shot mocha java across the bar, which she sipped. "How long until we get it?"

"These things take time, my dear Juniper," Quincy said with a wink. "I still have a few ingredients to source. But I promise you, it will be soon."

He leaned across the bar and lowered his voice conspiratorially. "Between you and me, we're lucky to have gotten our hands on some of these rare ingredients at all. I've had to call in quite a few favors."

"Yeah, I know. I owe you one, buddy." Juniper took a sip of her drink.

He leaned back and smiled at her. "You do. But don't worry. The potion will be ready before you know it."

"I hope so. I need to find out who killed Tiffany Davenport before everyone in Crescent Cove swears off my parties," Juniper said.

"I understand," Quincy said. "But, as I warned you before, the potion will only show you the last moments before Tiffany crossed over. It may not necessarily show you who killed her unless the angle of the mirror at that time captured the killer's face."

Juniper frowned. "But it's worth a try, right?"

"Of course," Quincy said. "It's always worth a try."

"Then the sooner I get the potion, the better."

"Patience is a virtue, Juni. We have to do it by the phases. Once the elixir is ready, we'll be there to do what has to be done with the mirror, but these things are very delicate. We can't rush this. The best answer I can give you is that we'll get it when we get it."

CHAPTER TEN

"When they got it" was only a few days later, but Juniper was ready to tear the walls down by that point.

Almost before Quincy's hand made contact with the door to knock, it swung inward, a harried-looking Juniper standing on the other side.

"It's about time!" she exclaimed, nearly dragging him inside. "I haven't had to fend off any little duckies in a few days, so we've got that going for us, but that doesn't mean Dear Desi doesn't have cards of his own up his sleeve."

Quincy slid a look at Tori, who was

following along, and she shrugged. "You know how she gets."

Following along behind Juniper, Quincy said, "June, you know this isn't a race, right? Or a test? You're not even qualified to work a murder case."

"And yet I have managed to solve how many at this point?" Juniper remarked as she speed walked through the mansion to the bathroom adjacent to the ballroom.

"Four," Tori said. "But who's counting?"

"Obviously, you are," Quincy remarked offhandedly, to which Tori snorted.

"Force of habit, I think."

"Stop yapping, you two," Juniper said. "It's distracting."

From what, Quincy couldn't be sure, unless she meant the moment. If that was the case, he had to suppress a chuckle. Only Juniper Holiday would get excited about going to the bathroom to perform a ritual spell. Or perhaps Quincy was just jaded about the magic of it all. He'd been performing spells since he was a boy, so this wasn't anything particularly exciting to him. He was getting a kick out of watching

Juniper act like a kid at Christmas, however.

Finally, they reached the bathroom. Juniper practically flung open the door and strode inside, careful to keep out of the way of the mirror, which, to Quincy's surprise, was covered in black cloth.

"I thought it might help if it was covered," she explained.

"It certainly won't hurt," Quincy said, tilting his head a bit to the side.

"Do we need to do this somewhere sacred or something?" Tori asked curiously.

"No," Quincy said, shaking his head. "I will need sunlight, however."

"Ballroom?"

"Direct sunlight," Quincy said, reaching to take the mirror off the wall. "It needs to be outside. Cripes, June. How much does this thing weigh?"

"I don't know," she said with a shrug. "I didn't pick it out or put it up. It's been here for generations."

Huffing with effort, Quincy managed to get the mirror out on the lawn without dropping it or straining any pertinent muscles on his body. It was a bit of a task putting it down without breaking it, but in the end he managed. None of them needed bad luck right now. He pulled the cloth away. A swath of blue sky was reflected in the mirror's face.

Taking a step back, he pulled a corked bottle from his jacket.

"Oooh, do we need to hold hands or speak an incantation out loud as a group?" Juniper asked with childish enthusiasm.

Quincy shook his head and unstopped the bottle. "Nope. The only one doing the chanting will be me unless you two know Latin."

"Nope," said Tori, while Juniper's admission was a bit more colorful.

"Dang! I knew I should have taken that elective in college!"

Chuckling, Quincy held his hand out over the mirror and tipped the bottle on its side so the contents poured out in a steady, continuous stream. In a whisper of breath, he began the incantation, asking for clarity and truth to be shown in the mirror's reflection. Before the stream was broken and the bottle began dripping the vestiges of the liquid, he ended the litany of Latin, righted the bottle, stoppered it, and returned it to his pocket.

He motioned Juniper and Tori closer and said, "Before you look into the mirror, think about what you wish to be revealed. It cannot show you anything other than truth and clarity. Focus on that and tell me what you see."

Both Tori and Juniper wore looks of concentration, though Juni's was perhaps a bit more intense. Then, together, they looked down into the pool of liquid covering the mirror. They watched with rapt attention.

"All you can see from this angle is Tiffany's hand," Tori said.

"And it looks like she's already dead," Juniper added then gasped. "Someone took her bracelet! The killer is also a thief!"

"What did you see?" Quincy asked the two women.

Tori looked up from the mirror, eyes wide. "Tiffany was lying on the ground. She must have just been strangled. Her hand was at her side, and another hand came into the picture and snatched the bracelet right off it!"

"But all we could see was the hands. Not the person. That bracelet snatcher is the killer, but we could only see a hand! What a rip-off." Juniper stood and stomped off toward the house.

Quincy watched her for a second then turned to Tori. "The vision only shows the moment the person passes over. Tiffany must have been breathing her last breath on the floor. You're lucky it showed anything at that angle though."

"I guess." Tori stood. A gust of wind blew her hair in her face, and a few strands got in her mouth, making her splutter. "Well, that came from out of nowhere."

Quincy wasn't so sure. He was no stranger to the paranormal, and rumor had it the Holiday mansion was haunted. It was possible one of the ghosts didn't like their disappointment in what they'd seen in the mirror.

He nodded toward the house. "What's next on the agenda? I know Juni's not going to stop until she gets answers."

Tori looked off in the direction Juniper had disappeared. "Back to the drawing board, probably. You're right about her not giving up. I just hope she manages to stay out of Stomper's crosshairs long enough to get the job done. Detective Mallard's job is kind of on the line too."

Quincy frowned. "Stomper?"

"Oh, uh, that's what everyone down at the precinct calls the chief of police because of the way he stomps around. Not where he can hear them, of course."

"Of course not," Quincy said with a chuckle.

Tori cocked her head to the side. "I'd invite you in for a spell, but if I know Juni, she's going to start blasting music in a minute, and we won't be able to hear ourselves think."

As if on cue, "I Want It All" by Queen started blasting through the speakers put up all through the place.

Shaking their heads at a certain amateur sleuth, Tori and Quincy went their separate ways.

The mirror lay outside on the lawn, the blue sky reflecting in the pool of magic left on its surface.

CHAPTER ELEVEN

*J*uniper was fuming. She had been hoping to see the face of the killer, but instead, all she got was a hand. A hand with no distinguishing marks. But now she knew the killer was really heartless. Strangling someone was bad enough, but to steal their bracelet while they were dying? That was just plain mean. But Juniper had to wonder… did the bracelet have some significance?

If it did, she had no idea what, and now she still didn't know who killed Tiffany Davenport. And she didn't have much to go on! She had been so fixated on the mirror potion being the answer she needed that she hadn't bothered to go about finding anything else to help her uncover the identity of the murderer.

"Ooooh, this is not how things were supposed to work out!"

Having Queen's "I Want It All" blaring at concert-level decibels in the background wasn't even helping her concentrate one bit. Nor was it calming her down as it should have, so Juniper picked up the remote and started flipping through her music. She didn't pay a bit of attention as the three-second snippets of tracks started, stopped, and started again. Instead, she kept clicking the button, waiting until a song started that fit her mood and the moment and the wretched state she found herself in after the potion fiasco.

Going from song to song, she danced around her office, dodging Ludo and Loki and picking up Finn and dancing with him in her arms while her brain tried to figure out the best place to start over with this whole Valentine's Day murder thing. She would be starting from the beginning instead of the end like she'd thought she would be. It was Queen's "We Will Rock You/We Are the Champions" combo that finally settled both her ruffled feathers and her frazzled soul enough to let her turn down the music again.

"I was beginning to wonder what was taking so long," Tori said from the doorway.

Juniper glanced up at her then back down at the paper in front of her. "Even you have to admit Quin's little magic mirror trick was more than a minor letdown."

Tori shrugged. "Maybe. He did say it would only capture the last thing."

"Yeah, well, I was hoping to see the killer. I'm going to have to start from the beginning on this murder thing now? And it's been days! Any clues that might have been lurking around here are probably all lost by now."

"Mmm, and that's what eats at you, isn't it?" Tori plopped down in a chair and curled her feet underneath her. Ludo jumped into her lap, and she stroked the cat's fur. "Or is it that you know Detective Mallard already has his ducks in a row and is probably closer to finding our killer than you now?"

Juniper held up the remote, her finger lingering like a threat over the volume button. "Mention that man's name again, and I won't be responsible for the consequences."

Tori laughed then scrambled from the chair, dumping Ludo on the floor. She grabbed the remote from Juniper's hand before her godmother could figure out what she was up to and promptly changed the song then hit the volume herself. Korn's "Twisted Transistor" poured through the mansion... which was probably why neither woman heard the bell or the knocking at the front door until the entire place suddenly fell silent.

Juniper glanced at Tori, who had been dancing around the room with her until the music died, then at Lionel, who had risen from the center of the floor, his expression resolute. "Detective Mallard is at the door, madam. Should I show him in?"

"Frankenfeathers? What is he doing here? Is that why you short-circuited my tunes?"

Juniper made a face, but before she could say anything more, Tori smacked her hand against her forehead. "Oh, God, I forgot he was coming by!" Tori tossed the remote onto Juniper's desk and hot-footed it to the door. "I'll get it."

"Victoria! Don't you dare!" Juniper raced after her, but she'd already opened the front door and was trying to force her breathing into a less accelerated pace even as Juniper skidded to a halt beside her.

"Traitor!" she hissed into Tori's ear, but Tori brushed the taunt away.

"Detective Mallard, I am sorry to keep you waiting out here. I forgot you were coming over, and the music was so loud…"

"How do you not have hearing problems, Miss Cooper? That was loud enough to wake the dead."

"Not entirely," Jacobi popped through the wall to say then patted his mouth to cover a yawn. "But she does get close sometimes."

CHAPTER TWELVE

After the initial interrogation from Juniper about why he was there, which he deftly avoided, Desmond found himself in the bathroom off the ballroom, which had been his goal for this little visit. Victoria knew, but she was the only one, and he wanted to keep it that way.

Desmond hadn't found much on Tiffany's phone. Just the usual pictures of her friends posing at the party and lots of selfies. Stomper was on him about this case. He didn't have much to go on, so he thought it might be worthwhile to take another look at the scene of the crime.

But so far, he had found nothing of interest, except that the mirror was a little crooked. But his team had already looked behind it and dusted it for prints, so that led him nowhere.

He was about to call his investigation done when one of the cats—the gray one he'd heard Tori call Finn—came racing into the bathroom. He ran around Desmond's legs and straight to a corner of the wall, where he started scratching.

"What in the world?" Desmond bent down to see a tiny opening in the corner. A mouse hole? Who knew a fancy mansion like this would have mice? Apparently, the cat knew, because he was snaking his paw into the hole as if trying to catch one.

"Watch out you don't get bit by one." Desmond said to Finn, who was paying no attention to him.

Finn pawed and batted and then jerked his paw out. Along with it came something shiny. Desmond bent down to inspect it and found, to his surprise, an earring.

Feeling a bit victorious, Desmond picked up the earring with a piece of tissue then straightened. Finn didn't seem the least bit impressed and simply trotted away while

Desmond inspected the earring. It was a stud earring with three diamonds in graduating sizes.

Could it have fallen off and rolled into the mouse hole during the struggle? It didn't match the gold hoops that Tiffany was wearing, which meant it could be from the killer.

More likely, though, it belonged to Juniper or Tori. He had no way of knowing how long it had been in there, but he doubted his forensics team would have looked in such a tiny opening.

He exhaled a short sigh of exasperation as he came to realize he was going to have to ask if the earring belonged to someone living in the house. He didn't want to bring Juniper's attention to the case any more than he strictly needed to, and this was sure to get the wheels in her head turning if the earring turned out to belong to someone else. There was nothing for it but to ask, though.

Unless…

He turned to look to see if he was alone and came face-to-face with none other than Felicity. His heart only thumped a couple of times at the sudden sight of her.

She smiled at him. "I do apologize for scaring you, Mr. Mallard. It was not my intention." She pointed at the piece of tissue in his hand and asked, "What's that you've got there?"

Desmond looked at the jewel between his fingers and then back at Felicity. Maybe he wouldn't have to show Juniper after all.

"Ms. Holiday's earring, I believe. Or perhaps Miss Cooper's. I found it in that little hole there."

Felicity floated closer, an inquisitive look on her ghostly features, and Desmond found himself opening his hand and letting her get a closer look at the jewelry without thinking. It wasn't like she could do anything with it, being incorporeal as she was.

"That's neither Juni's nor Tori's, I'm afraid," Felicity said, her big eyes seeming to peer into the deepest parts of him.

Just then, Jacobi popped into view, his innocent expression too contrived to be convincing. He'd definitely been spying on Desmond.

"I shall inform Mistress Juniper at once,"

he announced and disappeared before Desmond could say anything.

Biting back the growl of frustration forming in his throat, Desmond counted down the seconds until Juniper's arrival, knowing there was no point in trying to evade her. Her house was simply too large for him to escape in a timely manner.

"She's only curious, you know," Felicity said, reminding Desmond he was not alone.

"What do you mean?" he asked, his brows dipping in a slight frown.

"The mystery of it all is what pulls June in. She wants to find out who committed these atrocious crimes just as much as you do. Her reasons may not be yours, but she has them all the same."

Before he could inquire further, the door to the bathroom burst open, Felicity disappeared, and Juniper waltzed inside like she owned the place… which she did.

"I hear you found something, Duckbutt. An earring, to be precise. Lemme see it."

Desmond had the good sense and the timed reflexes to protect the evidence before Juniper could grab it. "It's an earring, Ms.

Holiday. That's all you need to know, and more importantly, all I'm going to tell you."

She narrowed her eyes at him. "You know that isn't mine. Or Tortellini's."

"Felicity told me as much."

"Good girl."

Juniper didn't take her eyes off of him.

Suddenly, Desmond felt like he was in an interrogation room and Stomper was staring him down himself.

"I'm not telling you anything else, Ms. Holiday."

"You don't have to," she said, giving a short shake of her head. "I have a list of suspects, same as you. They might not be the same people, but I'm betting at least one of them is. Maybe even two."

"Who would they be?"

She tsked and wagged her finger at him. "We're not sharing information, remember? You just rest easy knowing I won't bother you while you're out questioning your suspects."

Desmond's eyes narrowed. "You will stay out of this, Juniper Holiday. This is official police business and not something a civilian like you should be getting involved in, as if you didn't already know."

She cocked both her brow and her hip, her hands resting on the latter. "I know you're not telling me what I can and cannot do in my own home, Desmond Mallard."

"In your own home, you can do whatever you want, June. Outside of it, however, especially when it pertains to matters you have no business getting into, is a different matter entirely."

Her brow rose impossibly higher. "And that's how the last several murder cases were solved, is it? With me sitting at home, minding my own business? We both know the truth of that, Featherbutt."

Desmond, frustrated, pushed his fingers through his hair. Apparently, Juniper hadn't noticed that the police had solved those same cases with actual evidence that would hold up in court. Sure, she'd figured out who the killer was and gotten there a few minutes before them, but her methods would never ensure a conviction. Of course, Desmond knew that it would do no good to point any of this out to Juniper. She was stubborn. "Can you please just let me do my job, Ms. Holiday? For once?"

"I've never, not once, kept you from doing your job, Waddle-di-do."

Desmond returned to scowling. "I've had enough time to figure you out by now, Ms. Holiday. You're always planning something, always scheming to find loopholes you can exploit to do the very thing you're not supposed to do."

"If they weren't meant to be exploited," Juniper said, examining her nails, "then they wouldn't be loopholes. It's not my fault you rule followers get upset so easily. Make the fine print and legalese impenetrable, and you won't have so many problems with people like me."

Desmond put his hands on his hips. "Need I remind you both my job and your freedom are on the line, Ms. Holiday? Chief Gibbons isn't going to take kindly to your continued interference, Juniper. Especially when he all but forbade you from every crime scene in the jurisdiction after New Year's. He's breathing down my neck enough as it is."

A smile, simple and deadly as the serpent's

words to Eve in the Garden, slid onto Juniper's lips as easy as you please. It was then that Desmond knew further argument was futile, and this battle was lost. He offered up a prayer then and there that whatever crazy idea she had brewing in her brain wouldn't land either of them in water so hot they couldn't handle it.

She patted him on the arm, pearly whites gleaming, and said with a wink, "We both know what happens when someone tells me no, Detective. But you can rest assured your job won't come under fire from my visit to Delilah Fontaine. I may be a rebel, but even I know when to follow the rules… or at least make it look like I do."

CHAPTER THIRTEEN

Juniper had only gotten a glimpse of the earring, but she had a good memory. She rushed to her office and searched for pictures of her Valentine's Day party. Gina Dodd, a local journalist, always posted pictures on her blog right away, and the Valentine's party ones were right on the first page.

Loki hopped into her lap as she scrolled. Ludo tried to block the monitor, and Finn raced past her office door, chasing after something.

She scrolled through pictures, enlarging them to get a better look at each of the women's earrings. She started with Clarice

Belmont. Juniper hadn't forgotten the nasty looks she'd given to Tiffany when she'd won the grand prize. She'd clearly been jealous, but had she been jealous enough to kill?

Too bad Clarice was wearing long dangle heart earrings, not diamond studs. Juniper petted Loki's soft fur as she continued to peruse the photos.

"Aha!" Her exclamation startled Loki, and she flew off Juni's lap. But Juniper was already bolting out of her chair and grabbing her purse.

She'd found the killer!

Delilah Fontaine was wearing earrings that were an exact match to the one Mallard had found in the bathroom. Now all she had to do was get a confession, something which Juniper was getting pretty good at.

Juniper bopped her way out into the hallway, practically tripping over Finn, who meowed loudly, demanding to be petted as he stared up at her expectantly. At least he wasn't carrying a mouse in his mouth. Not one to deny the needy look in an animal's eye, especially not a cat's, Juniper bent and scooped the fluffy beast into her arms, hugging him close as she ran her fingers along his silky fur while continuing to dance and sing.

"Somebody's in a good mood," Tori said, coming down the stairs.

"Finn is definitely in a good mood," Juniper singsonged, twirling with Finn in her arms.

"Not who I was talking about, but I'll take it."

"I am also in a good mood," Juniper said, ruffling Finn's fur one more time before placing a kiss on top of his little kitty head and putting him down. She flashed a grin at Tori. "Ask me why."

Tori took the bait, asking as she walked by on her way to the kitchen, "Why are you in a good mood, June?"

Juniper smacked her hands together and snapped her fingers. "Because I've cracked the case, Tori-Bori!"

Tori glanced over her shoulder as she walked toward the kitchen. "That quick?"

"Uh-huh," Juniper said, falling into step behind her. "I love it when a plan comes together."

"So who did it?" Tori asked. They'd

reached the kitchen, where Sabrina was busy preparing dinner, and the smell that filled the room was downright mouthwatering.

She pointed a flour-encrusted finger at both of them. "Out, both of you, unless you've come to help me."

Both Juniper and Tori stopped in their tracks. It wasn't like Sabrina to order them out of the kitchen like this. They exchanged a quick side-eye with each other, then Tori said, "Uh… I was just coming to get some ice cream, Sabrina. I'm in a slump, and I need a sugar break."

Sabrina waved her hand, particles of flour falling from her fingers. "Fine, fine. Hurry up."

Juniper, however, was squinting mighty hard at the chef. This was beyond out of character for her. Sure, she'd been known to tell them to get out of her hair a few times, but not like this. Her actions were almost militant. She would even go so far as to say she was… possessed.

"Jacobi!" she hissed. "Are you doing this?"

Sabrina twitched.

Juniper's brows shot up to her hairline. "I

knew it! Jacobi, you stop possessing Sabrina this instant!"

A grumbling sigh that was very much reminiscent of the deceased man rumbled out of Sabrina. Jacobi-through-Sabrina looked at Juniper. "Just this one recipe, ma'am. Let me have this one recipe, please."

Juniper snapped her fingers. "Now!"

With a beleaguered sigh, Jacobi extricated himself from Sabrina's form. Sabrina, bless her, went about preparing the food as though nothing had happened. Juniper made a mental note to have a serious talk with Jacobi about possessing people without their permission as soon as she finished gloating to Tori about catching the killer.

Tori didn't ask about the strange exchange in the kitchen until they were out of it and headed back upstairs. "Was that—?"

"Jacobi. Yes. Somehow, he managed to find a way to possess Sabrina."

"You mean they can do that?" Tori asked, wide-eyed.

"Apparently," Juniper said, following her into her room and shutting the door behind them. In his place beside Tori's desk, completely covered in a pile of blankets he insisted on keeping in his little bed, Barclay, Tori's chihuahua mix, gave a muffled bark at having his sleep interrupted. His head poked up to disrupt the covers enough to reveal his snout and his soulful chocolate-brown eyes. He sniffed then snorted and dropped his head back down, content to go back to sleep now that he knew who had awoken him.

"I knew they could do that," Juniper continued. "Possess people, I mean. But I've never seen them do it."

"Maybe he's been practicing and you just didn't know about it," Tori offered, going over to her bed and plopping down on the end of it, crossing her legs beneath her.

"It's possible, I suppose," Juniper said, her brow creased in thought. "But we're not talking about that right now. I figured out who killed Tiffany!"

"Do tell," Tori said around a mouthful of ice cream.

"Delilah Fontaine!"

"How do you figure it was her?"

"Remember when I used Gina Dodd's blog to solve the last murder?"

Tori nodded, looking a little skeptical.

"Well, it came in handy again." Juniper explained how she'd zoomed in on the pictures of the party and found that Delilah was wearing earrings just like the one that Mallard found. She clapped her hands together when she finished and beamed at Tori.

"Oka-aa-y," Tori said, drawing out the "a" and then licking the spoon. "But she might not be the only one with earrings like that, and there's no guarantee that the owner of the earring is the killer. I mean, she could have simply lost the earring when she used the bathroom or lost it somewhere else and one of the cats batted it in there."

Juniper made a face. "Don't be such a killjoy."

Tori laughed. "I just don't want you to get ahead of yourself. I know this must give you some sort of thrill, June, but you have to remember these are real people with real lives, and if you go handing out accusations left and right, well…"

Juniper put her hands on her hips. "Does

this have something to do with Detective Duckbutt?"

"No. Not really." Tori played with her ice cream. "Well, maybe. You know his boss is on his case about you interfering, and if you go around accusing people, it could cost him his job."

"Or if I find the killer," Juniper said, then her expression softened at the look on Tori's face. "Look, I don't want to get him into trouble. But I have this compulsion to solve these murders. I mean, it does reflect on me that they keep happening at my parties. But this time, I'll be discreet and hand my evidence over to Mallard."

Tori's eyes narrowed. "You mean like the evidence we saw in the mirror?"

Juniper sighed. She'd thought about telling Mallard, but he hadn't taken the fact that he could see ghosts well at first, and getting him to accept that an enchanted mirror had evidence that would help solve the case didn't seem likely. "Yes, that too."

"Okay, but I still think you need proof before you can declare someone is the killer. Undeniable proof."

Juniper stared at her for a long minute, her eyes turning beady. Then they snapped wide with sudden realization. "You mean I should go talk to Delilah. Get her to confess. See if she has the bracelet that the killer took."

Tori nodded slowly. "That's exactly what I mean."

CHAPTER FOURTEEN

Twenty minutes later, Tori and Juniper were knocking on the door to Delilah's apartment.

Delilah answered the door, wearing yoga pants and a long shirt. She looked surprised to see them. "Hi. Can I help you?"

"We're here to congratulate you on the prize you won at the Valentine's Day party and apologize that it got cut short because of the murder."

Delilah looked skeptical but opened the door wider to invite them in. The apartment was small but tidy. The front door opened to an open area that had a living room and kitchen.

The kitchen had a small table set for two near a window that overlooked the quaint Crescent Cove downtown area. The living room was clean, with an oversized leather sofa and armchair that was soft and worn. A colorful woven rug added interest to the worn wooden floors.

The smell of freshly brewed coffee wafted out of the kitchen.

"Thank you so much for coming by. That was really sweet of you." Delilah gestured for them to sit. "Can I get you some coffee?"

Tori shook her head. "No thanks. We can't stay. We just wanted to make sure you were okay after what happened."

Delilah sighed. "I'm still in shock, to be honest. I can't believe someone died."

Juniper nodded sympathetically. "I know. It's been hard for all of us, but it must be really hard on you since you were so close."

Delilah looked confused. "Close? We weren't really that close."

"You weren't? I thought you hung with that crowd. I'm sure I've seen you with Clarice Belmont and Emma Porter." Juniper was getting impatient to get to the confession.

Looking around the room, she wondered how Delilah could afford diamond earrings. She wasn't rich like the other girls, but maybe she was trying to keep up with them. And maybe she was jealous of what they had. That might give her a motive to kill.

Delilah stiffened, her chin raised slightly. "Clarice is my cousin. But the truth is that I never really fit in with that crowd."

Juniper nodded, feigning sympathy for a second, then blurted out, "Is that why you killed Tiffany?"

Even Tori blinked at her blunt, in-your-face question, but Juniper didn't. She held Delilah Fontaine's gaze until the younger woman looked away, a mist of tears in her eyes.

"Do you really think I would do something like that? Truly?" She glanced back and forth from Juniper to Tori then covered her face with her hands. "Wait, is that what the police think?"

"What old Featherpants thinks and what we think have nothing to do with each other," Juniper said. "That being said, you should know we found your diamond earring in my ballroom bathroom. The same bathroom that Tiffany Davenport was found murdered in."

Delilah's hand flew to her left ear. "Oh no."

"That's right," Juniper continued. "I wonder how you can afford expensive earrings like that. Maybe you stole them and Tiffany found out, so you had to silence her."

"What? No. You're way off track there. Clarice bought me those earrings so I wouldn't embarrass her by looking like the poor cousin when our families visited Paris."

"That must have stung to be thought of as the poor cousin. I bet you resented Clarice and her friends. Especially Tiffany."

"Maybe a little. Especially since she wouldn't get me the heart-shaped ones. Clarice and the cool-girl gang each had a pair, but she said it was only for them. They liked to get the same things… to show everyone that they were the in crowd and the rest of us were out."

Juniper leaned forward in her chair, certain she was about to get a confession. "I bet that stung even worse. You wanted to be with the in crowd. You've been harboring a resentment for a decade now."

Delilah made a face. "Hardly. Maybe in high school I was hurt, but now, I see them for what they are. Shallow and mean. I wouldn't waste my time killing one of them, but if you ask me, plenty of people had something against them back then. Melissa McCool, Deb Schwann, Tracy Muller, Edie Smith… just about any girl in high school that got bullied by them. But that was a long time ago. Why would anyone still hold a grudge?" Delilah held her hand out, and Juniper noticed she wore no bracelets on either wrist. That didn't mean she didn't have Tiffany's bracelet stashed away, though. "Anyway, I did lose an earring, but not because I struggled while killing Tiffany. Are you here to return it?"

"We couldn't if we wanted to, Delilah. It's in lockup at the Crescent Cove precinct in town, under Detective Mallard's watchful eye."

Delilah's cheeks flushed, and she closed her eyes. "What? Why? Why do things like this always happen to me?"

Juniper's eyelashes fluttered, not in surprise

but in an effort to keep the flash of triumph over being right from beaming into the room. "Well, when you murder someone, you can hardly expect to get away with it."

"Wait, what? No, no, no!" Delilah shook her head to further emphasize the denial. "I did not kill Tiffany. What I meant was, I am going to have to explain how the earring got in your bathroom to the police. It's ... it's so embarrassing! I never wanted it to get out."

Juniper glanced at Tori. She could tell Tori was starting to believe Delilah, though she wasn't sure why. Most murderers did deny doing it. Still, she supposed she should see what the girl had cooked up as a lie. "Why don't you tell us how your earring ended up in the bathroom, then."

Delilah closed her eyes. After an awkward moment, she said, "You both remember Anthony Durrie, don't you? Tall, blond curls, hottie who works at RarelyDone?"

"Oh my good lord, yes," Tori said, fanning herself. "That man doesn't even know how dangerous it is for him to go out, does he?"

"Apparently not, since he was at Juniper's party. We danced a few times. Had a couple drinks... or three. We—ah—slipped off into a quiet little corner, but then Tony decided we maybe needed a bit more privacy."

Giving Juniper an "I-told-you-so" look, Tori made a cooing sound then said, "You two must have really been into each other, huh?"

Delilah's face went red. "The closest room we knew of with a door that had a lock was the bathroom in the ballroom..."

"Oh..." Juniper made a face, picturing Delilah and Anthony in her bathroom, doing things that would make Delilah lose an earring. But why would Delilah lie about that? It would be easy enough to verify. "I see. Did you happen to see Tiffany after you were done, ah... using the facilities?"

Delilah's face was bright red. "No. Sorry."

"Okay, then." Juniper stood up. She hadn't gotten the confession she wanted, but maybe she'd gotten a step closer to solving the case. "I guess we'd better get going. Have a nice day, and try to stay out of people's bathrooms."

CHAPTER FIFTEEN

"*L*et me guess, you want to go straight to RarelyDone to confirm Delilah's alibi with Anthony," Tori said when they were in the car.

"Bingo! And get a steak. I'm starving." Juniper weaved her sporty car through traffic as she headed to the steakhouse. "I'm not believing Delilah that easily, though I do agree it would be dumb for her to lie about something so easily verified."

Juniper cut a hard right and pulled into an empty space near the steakhouse. As usual, the sound of her car's engine growling had eyes and heads turned her way as far as the eye could see.

Putting the car in park, she killed the ignition and got out, shut the door, and walked around the nose of the car and onward to RarelyDone. Tori followed right behind her. Juniper was looking forward to checking out Delilah's alibi but even more so to sitting down and having a nice meal with her goddaughter at one of her favorite restaurants.

"Well, well. Look what the cat dragged in. Haven't seen you around these parts in a good little while, Juniper. You want me to tell Victor to throw your usual on the grill, or are you going to surprise me and order something different this time?"

"Garrett, I am a creature of habit. I'll take the usual, thank you. Tori is the weirdo who has to try everything on the menu at least a dozen times before she decides something is her favorite."

"Ha, funny, June. It's not my fault you're boring. Variety is the key to living a full life," Tori retorted.

"You're preaching to the choir, sweetie," Juniper responded, flicking a glance at Tori over her shoulder.

Garrett laughed. "Never a dull moment

with you two. You want a booth or at the bar?"

"Bar," they answered in unison.

"Follow me."

They did so. Once they were seated, a routine rapid-fire ribbing between the guys manning the grill, which could be seen from the bar, and Juniper commenced, with Tori chiming in with some of the best one-liners.

Tori and June had become close friends with the staff at RarelyDone when they'd discovered one night—during a full moon—that many of them were werewolves. Not many in town knew about that, and Juniper and Tori were sworn to secrecy.

In record time, their food was brought out and placed in front of them with a flourish from none other than the grill master himself, and then it was chow time. Not much was said at this time, as both women were busy enjoying their meal. Eventually, as their stomachs got fuller, conversation picked up.

"You know, Tor," Juniper began, sipping from her glass of iced sweet tea with lemon, "I think I'm going to take a break from this murder business."

Tori cleared her throat. "Maybe a poor choice of words, there, June."

"You know what I mean," Juniper said, rolling her eyes. "Finding the killers and whatnot."

"Don't tell me you're throwing in the towel. Just because Delilah probably didn't do it doesn't mean someone didn't. You just have to reassess. Take a step back. Look at it from a different point of view."

Juniper arched a brow. "Now you're going to hype me up?"

Tori leveled a look at her. "June. Come on."

"I know. And no, I'm not throwing in the towel. Far from it, kiddo. No, I just think I need to take a brain break is all. Not think about it for a day or two and come back to it with fresh eyes."

"So basically what I just said."

"Shut up, brat."

Tori laughed, and Juniper smiled.

"So what are you going to do in the meantime?"

"Easter isn't that far away. I've still got the

rest of the scavenger hunt to plan. I've been neglecting it, I'm afraid."

Tori tsked.

"I know. Terrible of me." Juniper sighed. "I could—"

"Hold that thought," Tori interrupted. "There's Tony. You wanna ask him the dirty details, or should I?"

Juniper turned to look where Tori was surreptitiously pointing. Tony was at a table, taking an order. "Delilah was not kidding. That man is a stunner."

"He is, indeed. You got two seconds to get off your stool before I waylay him on his way back to the kitchen and ask him."

"Have at it, kid."

Tori slipped off the stool without a second thought and wound her way through the maze of booths and tables before stopping to linger beside a large potted plant near the kitchen. Tori wasted no time in getting Tony's attention as he passed by. The two talked for a while, and Juniper turned back to her steak.

"Alibi confirmed," Tori said, hopping back onto the stool. "The deed went down just like

Delilah said. Funnily enough, even Tony seemed embarrassed to admit it."

"Wouldn't you be?" Juniper asked, raising both brows.

"He asked if you had security cameras in the place."

Juniper nearly snorted her tea out her nose. "What did you tell him?"

"I told him he *probably* didn't need to worry about his activities ending up on cable somewhere."

Juniper's jaw nearly hit the floor. "You did not!"

"I did so."

Juniper cackled. "You are a fiend, Victoria! A devilish little fiend."

Tori grinned and raised her glass to Juniper in a toast. "I learned from the best."

Loud laughter drew their attention to a secluded booth in the corner.

"Hey, isn't that Clarice Belmont?" Juniper asked.

Tori turned in that direction. "Yeah, I'd recognize that blond dye job anywhere. Looks like she's on a date with someone."

"Huh, guess she's making good use of the

guest certificate she won at the Valentine's party."

"Hopefully, she's making the guy pay." Tori squinted and craned her neck in Clarice's direction then grabbed Juniper's arm. "Look at her wrist!"

As Juniper watched, Clarice put her hand up to fluff her hair. On her wrist was the heart bracelet, just like the one they had seen taken from Tiffany by the killer.

CHAPTER SIXTEEN

It pained Juniper to hand over their information about seeing Clarice wearing Tiffany's bracelet to Mallard, but Tori had insisted. Juniper could see that Tori was afraid the guy would lose his job, and as much as Juniper liked to mess with him, she really didn't want that to happen.

Whether or not he would believe them about seeing the killer take the bracelet in the enchanted mirror and how he would present that to a jury was another matter. But that was his problem now. Juniper had done all she could.

She hummed a tune as she sat at her desk, sipping a coffee Anne brought in while she worked on putting together scavenger hunt clues for the Easter treasure hunt. There was no doubt in her mind plenty of Covians would attend the event. Despite the recent spate of murders at her place, well, there was simply too much fun to be had—not to mention a sweet little ten-thousand-dollar-check-filled prize egg to find. Some might think it was over the top, but Juniper Holiday never did things by half measure. If there was a prize to be had, well, it might as well be worth something.

She was surprised DuckyMuck hadn't come by to interrogate her and put a damper on her findings. She assumed Tori would call him—Juniper certainly wasn't going to make the call—but Victoria had the weirdest fascination for the guy.

"Kids and their strange tastes in men." Juniper shook her head, set her cup aside, then leaned over to scratch Loki behind the ears. "Some things, I don't think I'll ever understand."

"I'm quite certain your parents must have felt the same way, June," Lionel said when he popped into the room through the French doors leading out to the garden. "If I recall correctly, your fascination for a certain gent was not one highly approved of."

Juniper dropped the pen and slid back her chair as thoughts of *him* bubbled up. She pushed them away as quickly as they came—she was in too good a mood to go down that sad lane of memories. She picked up her cup of coffee again then eyed the ghost through narrowed eyelids. "Shouldn't believe everything you hear, Lion-O. Gossip is half lies and half not true but one hundred percent malicious—in my experience, at least."

"Are you saying mean things about Detective Mallard again, Juniper?" Tori asked, having come into the room in time to catch the last few words of her godmother's contribution to the barely started conversation.

"Nope. Of course not, Tori-bori. I was just cautioning Lionel here how some things are better left unsaid—like the truth about how that Delilah girl's earring happened to be in my bathroom."

Tori laughed. "I've never known you to be so sensitive to others' feelings."

Juniper shrugged. "I'm not that bad.

Speaking of bad, did you call old Featherbutt?"

"I did, actually, and Desmond wasn't the least bit surprised to hear about our discoveries."

Juniper frowned. "Did you tell him about the enchanted mirror part?"

"Yep. He seemed to take it in stride, which was a surprise to me." Tori made herself comfortable on the sofa and sipped at her own cup of coffee before asking, "What have you been up to this morning? I mean, since you're crying off playing Columbo and all... at least for the time being."

"I've been writing clues for the scavenger hunt and ordering a pool full of Jell-O to be delivered a day in advance. Eww. Just realized the weather could be warm in April. Do you think it'll be melted by morning?"

Tori gave Juniper a look that said she thought her godmother was just barely this side of sanity. "I still can't believe you're doing that, June. You do realize the job you're creating for our pool guy, right? I pity him having to clean the thing after."

"He'll be fine, Tor. I'll pay him extra.

What about you? Why are you up early? Got a character bugging you?"

"It's not early. It's after eleven, June. Wow, you must have been into your planning this morning."

Juniper shrugged, letting her think she'd been down here for hours, but in truth, she'd only been in her office since about ten thirty. She'd awakened around five thirty in the morning but elected to stay in her room with the cats. She didn't want Tori to know she was worried about the case. Yes, they'd found the killer... or so it seemed. But something didn't sit right.

"The only way to get it done is to actually sit down and do it, you know. Did the Duckster say anything? Mention other clues that point to Clarice? I'm sure he has leads old Stompity Stomp won't let him share with me, but he might make an exception for you."

Tori gave her a blank look then shook her head. "Desmond didn't really have anything to share, June."

"Well, I'm sure he knows what to do," Juniper said, pretending a loss of interest. "In the meantime, why don't we go out to the gazebo? I want to look over the framing and such to find the best place to hide a clue."

Tori seemed not to have heard her. She was staring off at nothing and picking at the handle of her cup while doing so. "Even so, I still feel like something isn't right. That bit with Delilah and the earring was a little too easy, and Clarice wearing the bracelet so boldly out in public. Maybe there's another clue in the bathroom we missed."

"There is another clue, but it's not in the bathroom," Lionel said, though only Juniper could hear him. "In fact, it's right in front of your faces. Ms. Holiday, are you sure you really don't see her?"

Juniper's brows snapped downward in a frown. "What? See who? Lionel, what are you going on about now?"

The ghost dipped his vaporous head to one side. "Her. She's right there. Came whooshing through the outer wall about five minutes ago. Poor thing. She's new and obviously having trouble, but she'll figure things out soon. Should I ask her to stay here or take her upstairs to have a lie-down in Felicity's room?"

"Who?" Juniper demanded as the faintest scent of lavender wafted around her. "Lionel, call me crazy if you want, but I don't see anyone but your ghostly self and Tori-Bori. If there's something else I should be noticing, I'm afraid I don't see it."

"June, you really have to stop talking to them when I'm in the room," Tori insisted. "Sounds like a crazy, one-sided conversation."

"Tiffany Davenport, Ms. Holiday. Well, her noncorporeal form. She's a ghost now that she's left your world, but…"

"A ghost? Tiffany's a ghost, and she's here? I don't understand, Lionel. If she's here, then why can't I see her?"

Tori's snort was not as silent as she'd meant it to be. "A question I often ask myself, June."

Juniper set her cup down and hurried across the room to where Lionel had motioned. "Put a sock in it, Tori, and call the Duckster. Now. Lionel says Tiffany is here now, and if I can't see her, maybe he can."

CHAPTER SEVENTEEN

Desmond stared at his phone screen for a moment after the call ended. He felt a mix of things at Tori's request. The fact that Juniper had been the one to request his presence at her home was stunning enough; that she wanted his help was very nearly overkill.

If he hadn't come to know the two as well as he had over the past several months, he would say it was a prank done in bad faith. But since he did know them and the often-times strange things that happened at the mansion—having experienced a good deal of it himself—he pocketed his phone and headed for his car.

"Where ya goin', Boss?" Nichols asked as he came out of his office.

"Out" was Desmond's succinct reply, the word clipped.

Nichols may have said something else, but Desmond was too far away to hear him. Plus, he pretended he didn't hear him. He didn't need the distraction or the questions. And he certainly didn't need anyone knowing where he was going.

He couldn't deny he was curious as he made the drive to Juniper's place. According to Tori, there was a matter that only he could help with. She hadn't explained more than that over the phone, and the questions that came to Desmond's mind because of it were… exciting. He couldn't remember the last time he had felt this way in regard to his work.

Before he knew it, he was pulling to a stop in front of the mansion. After putting the car in park and turning off the ignition, he stepped out, buttoning his coat as he made his way up the steps. He didn't even bother ringing the bell, as the door was wrenched open right as he reached it, as he figured it would be. If they were expecting him, they made it a habit to anticipate his arrival with frightening accuracy.

"Good, you're here," Tori said, wrapping her arm around his as he stepped over the threshold. "Juni's waiting for you in her office."

"I feel like I'm in trouble," he mumbled.

Tori laughed. "Relax, Des. She's not going to yell at you. She really does need your help."

"That is almost more frightening than being yelled at."

Again, Tori laughed, but she said nothing else as she led him to Juniper's office. Once there, she shut the door behind them.

Juniper, he saw, was standing near the bookcases on the far wall, talking to Lionel as she walked in a circle around a spot he indicated, her face a mask of concentration. "You're *sure* she can hear me, Lionel?"

"Yes, ma'am," Lionel said, sounding truly put-upon.

"And she's talking to you?"

Lionel nodded. "In bits and pieces, yes. I told you, she's a young ghost. She has not managed to get control of her abilities yet."

Juniper clicked her tongue and crossed her

arms, cocking her hip to the side as she rested her weight on her leg. Her brows dipped in a frown. "Daggum it."

Tori cleared her throat, releasing her hold on his arm as she did so. Desmond missed the feeling immediately. "Desmond's here, June."

Her sharp eyes turned on him faster than he was ready for. She raised one hand and motioned him over with two fingers. "Come here."

Desmond walked forward until he was standing next to Lionel. "What seems to be the problem, Ms. Holiday? Victoria didn't exactly give me details."

"That's because I told her not to," Juniper said. "Do you see anything in front of you? Specifically in the space between us?"

Desmond's brows lowered slightly as he wondered what she was getting at, but knowing she would snap at him if he pressed for further explanation, he examined the space she mentioned and looked back at her. "I see nothing."

Juniper cursed, her shoulders slumping.

Something began to materialize right before his eyes. "Wait," he said, focusing on it.

"Something is starting to appear." He flicked his eyes away from the strange formation to momentarily focus on Juniper. "Should I be worried?"

"No," Lionel answered in Juniper's stead. "It is Tiffany Davenport, Detective Mallard. Your victim. She has been trying to manifest for Juniper for quite some time but hasn't managed it." His bushy ghostly eyebrows lowered. "That she is becoming visible to you tells me she must somehow be connected to you in some way."

Desmond didn't know how to respond to that, so he stayed quiet, watching in awe as Tiffany's form became clearer. The scent of lavender was familiar. Hadn't he smelled that same scent in his office?

She smiled a relieved smile. "Detective," she said, her voice sounding wavery. "I've been trying to contact you."

"I'm sorry," Desmond said. "I... don't know why you weren't able to."

"It may be that the mansion amplifies what makes us ghosts, Detective," Lionel explained. "It is situated on an ancient ley line, and we draw our power from that. Since

Tiffany was murdered here, that is perhaps why she is only visible to you here. Her body is tied to this place."

"I don't know the semantics," Tiffany said to Desmond. Her words were broken up like a bad phone connection. "I've… trying … message …."

"Well, I'm here now. What is it you wanted to tell me, Miss Davenport?"

"Not… Clarice… jealous… heart drain…"

"What?" Desmond asked in a rush, his heart suddenly pounding at the thought of the victim herself giving him a clue.

Tiffany's mouth moved, but no more words came. Then her form began to fade from view.

Desmond looked to Lionel for an explanation.

"She is a young ghost, unable to hold onto her form for long. With practice, she will be able to perfect it, but it will take time."

Desmond nodded.

Across from him, Juniper cleared her throat. "You wanna tell me what she said, Detective? 'Cause I didn't hear a word of it."

CHAPTER EIGHTEEN

"It was quite garbled, but she said something like 'not-something-Clarice-something-jealous-something-heart-drain.'"

Juniper made a face. "Huh, what does that even mean? Is she giving us a clue about how to nail Clarice as the killer? She mentioned Clarice, and the bracelet has hearts on it."

"If so, it's rather cryptic," Desmond said. "And I doubt the jury is going to be convinced by the fact that you saw the killer snatch the bracelet in a mirror that you'd had enchanted with some sort of spell."

"Good point. And I suppose they don't tend to put much stock in clues from ghosts.

We need something more solid than what we've got," Juniper said. At least Desmond believed they'd seen the killer take the bracelet in the mirror. "This is bad. Real bad. You know the killer but can't bring her in."

Desmond had been silent for several minutes, but Juniper's words seemed to snap him—almost—from a sort of dazed trance. His mind was working normally now, but the look he turned on her was still the kind where he saw her almost without seeing... the he-looked-right-through-me kind of gaze, but his words were clear. "So we find evidence."

His words were spoken in such a deadpan tone, Juniper cracked a laugh.

"You okay over there, Duckman? Maybe Tortellini needs to whack you upside the head or something. Scramble your brains a bit to knock you out of your haze."

Juniper glanced at her desk and then snapped her fingers. "I've got it! We can't show them an enchanted mirror, but we can show them pictures from the party."

Desmond and Tori clustered around while Juniper brought up Gina Dodd's blog. "Gina posts pictures of everything. See? Here is me announcing the winner of the contest."

"June, we're not looking for you. We're looking for evidence. Like that!" Tori pointed to the screen, which was a picture of Tiffany smiling at the camera. "Zoom in on her wrist."

Juniper zoomed in to reveal the heart bracelet.

"Aha!" Juniper said. "That proves that Tiffany had the bracelet. Now all we need to do is find out a reason for the police to bring Clarice in and hope she is wearing it."

"Not so fast." Tori pointed to another picture. This one was of the brat pack—Clarice, Tiffany, Lacey, and Emma. They were all holding up valentine cards. "Zoom in on their wrists."

Juniper did as told. "Oh no." All four of them were wearing the heart bracelet.

"Darn!" Tori said. "Delilah said they had twin accessories to show they were a clique, remember?"

Juniper nodded. "She seemed jealous because Clarice wouldn't get her the heart earrings that they all had."

Desmond had been standing there quietly watching. "Jealous? That's what Tiffany's ghost said."

Juniper looked at him. "Delilah's earring was in the bathroom, and she sounded jealous."

"But she has an alibi with Anthony," Tori said.

Desmond shook his head. "Not an alibi, not really. He did say they were in there together, but that doesn't mean she wasn't also in there at another time, and they certainly weren't in there together when Tiffany was killed."

"Good point!" Juniper said. "She could have even gone in with Anthony on purpose to create a reason for her to be in there other than killing Tiffany."

"And we know she likes hot guys. Maybe she was not just jealous that Tiffany was one of the 'in crowd' girls, but she was also jealous she won the date with Adrien!"

"Her earring could have gotten lost when she killed Tiffany, but how would we prove that?" Juniper was disappointed. "We're still at square one."

"Not necessarily," Desmond said. "The other thing Tiffany's ghost said was 'drain.'"

"You mean something went down the drain?" Juniper jumped up from her chair. "Something that we can use as real evidence to prove Delilah killed her!"

Juniper hurried toward the ballroom, shouting out instructions for Terence to bring tools that one could disassemble pipes with.

"I don't know if we should do this, June," Tori confessed as they headed for the ballroom. "Have you ever removed drainpipes before? I haven't. Never had a reason to. What if we mess something up in there?"

"Don't worry so much, Tori, darling. Just pop them loose and see what you find in every area you can actually reach. We'll worry later about putting things back together. We have plenty of bathrooms."

Terrence appeared and started handing things to Tori and Desmond—a set of screwdrivers, a pair of C-shaped pliers, and a pipe wrench.

"This should be everything you need." Terence bowed and left them to it.

Juniper turned in a circle and frowned.

"We need some demolition music."

The words had barely left her mouth before the screaming first notes of Poison's "Tearin' Down the Walls" echoed through the mansion. Desmond shot Tori a look. "Does she do *any*thing without a playlist?"

♥

"Well, that was gross," Juniper said two hours later as she washed the muck off the small gold heart that had been trapped in the elbow of the drainpipe to her sink.

"What is it?" Desmond asked.

Juniper held the tiny heart up. "It's a twenty-four-carat gold heart. It was on top of one of the chocolates I gave as a runner's-up prize."

"Maybe that's why Tiffany's ghost said 'heart,'" Desmond mused.

Tori looked at the small gold piece. "So, the killer ate chocolates? And then what? Killed her? Seems like an odd thing to do."

"Maybe Delilah lured her in here with one of the chocolates." Juniper switched her gaze from the heart to Desmond. "The sash had that smudge of chocolate on it. I was hoping it was blood."

"Me too," Desmond said. "At least blood has DNA that could point to a person. Chocolate smudges and gold hearts don't really help us in that department."

"But you said you could narrow down the chocolate by the ingredients," Juniper said.

Desmond shrugged. "Somewhat. We were able to determine the smudge came from chocolates made with the same recipe that they use at Decadent Delights, but that's hardly useful since there were chocolates all over your entire party."

It was true—Juniper had provided chocolates in little netting bags at each place setting, and the food tables had had three-tiered silver trays loaded with chocolates.

"But I had all my chocolates flown in from Belgium," Juniper said. She shut off the tap then dried her hands and the little heart with the towel Tori handed her. "The only chocolates here that were from Decadent Delights were the ones in the runner's-up prize that Tracy Muller won."

"So what do you think? Delilah stole Tracy's chocolates, killed Tiffany, and then stole her bracelet?" Tori asked.

Juniper gnawed on her bottom lip. "Maybe. Everyone knew those chocolates had real gold hearts. Could she have used it somehow to get Tiffany into the bathroom?"

"Perhaps, but we need more than guesses." Desmond let out a sigh of disappointment. "We need some sort of link, physical evidence or a witness."

"What if we could get Tracy to tell us she gave Delilah one of those chocolates? Would that be enough to get a warrant to search Delilah's place? If you found the heart bracelet there, it could be the physical evidence you need."

Desmond pressed his lips together. "Perhaps. If Tiffany's DNA is on the bracelet, that could work. We have pictures of her wearing it at the party, and the log at the morgue will show it wasn't on her wrist when she was brought in."

"Perfect. Then I think I know exactly what to do," Juniper said, the wheels in her head clicking and turning as she thought up a plan.

CHAPTER NINETEEN

Tracy Muller lived in a small ranch house at the edge of the cove. The siding was white, and the shutters were green. There was a detached garage at the end of the driveway. Juniper parked in front of it and got the giant heart-shaped box of chocolates out of the passenger seat.

The chocolates were her excuse to pay Tracy a visit, and she'd come alone, thinking that if she brought Tori, the two of them might be a bit intimidating.

She rang the bell, and Tracy answered, looking surprised to see Juniper.

Juniper held out the box. "Hi, Tracy. I

forgot to give you these at the party. They're soft centers."

Tracy smiled and took the box. "Thank you so much, Juniper. You didn't have to do that."

"Of course I did," Juniper replied. She got the sense that Tracy was about to close the door, but Juniper couldn't have that. She had questions to ask. "I hope you are doing okay after the horrible incident at my party."

"Yes. I'm fine." Tracy must have noticed Juniper eyeing the inside of the house. "Would you like a cup of coffee?"

"I'd love one. Coffee goes great with these chocolates." Juniper handed her the box and pushed her way in.

The house was cozy and inviting, with warm wood floors and plenty of natural light streaming in through the large windows.

Tracy led her to a small kitchen and put a kettle of water on to boil. "Have the police gotten any leads on the killer?"

Juniper couldn't believe her luck. Just the subject she wanted to talk about. "They have a few, but nothing solid. I can't imagine who would have wanted Tiffany dead. Can you?"

"No. Such a shame." Tracy busied herself with putting the coffees on the table and opening the box of chocolates.

"We did find something odd at the murder scene, and I was wondering if you gave any of your chocolates to Delilah Fontaine."

Tracy sat down opposite Juniper, and the extra-long sleeves of her sweater covered half her hands as she wrapped them around her mug of coffee. "Why do you ask that? Is she a suspect?"

Juniper looked at her out of the corner of her eye. "It's not really my place to say... but..."

"I did share some chocolates with her. I shared with everyone." Tracy sounded cautious.

The back of Juniper's neck prickled. There was something off. She wasn't exactly sure what, but her intuition told her to be cautious.

"Which flavors did Delilah take?" Juniper asked.

Tracy's eyes narrowed. "Umm... caramel and dark chocolate."

That was odd. The gold hearts had been

on the nut clusters. Suddenly, Juniper had a bad feeling.

"You mean like these?" Juniper pointed to one of the chocolates in the box.

"No, these." Tracy raised her hand to point. Her sweater slid up her arm, and a heart bracelet slid down on her wrist. The same heart bracelet that Tiffany had been wearing.

Juniper sucked in a breath. Tracy wasn't one of the "in gang," so she shouldn't have that bracelet, unless...

She looked up and met Tracy's cold gaze.

"You ask too many questions," Tracy said.

"That's me! I'm nosey. Everyone says so. Well, I guess I should be going." Juniper pushed up from the table, but Tracy was faster and blocked her exit.

"You didn't give any chocolates to Delilah, did you?" Juniper figured she might as well satisfy her curiosity while she was trying to figure out how to get away from Tracy.

"Nope."

"But you did give one to Tiffany."

"Yep." Tracy kept her eyes on Juniper as

she reached behind her and grabbed an apron.

Juniper thought that was a strange thing to do. What was she planning on doing with the apron? Juni looked around for a weapon she could use. Too bad she was in the doorway with no knives or heavy objects conveniently behind her. A little ghostly help like she'd gotten when she'd faced off against the last killer would have been welcome, but she didn't see any ghostly swirls. She was on her own.

"Why did you kill her, Tracy?" Juniper asked.

Tracy's expression turned evil. "She was always the winner, and I was the loser. Tiffany and her little gang got all the cute guys, all the good opportunities."

"That must have been frustrating." Juniper tried to sound sympathetic.

"It sure was. And then they would throw it in everyone's faces with their matching purses, earrings, and bracelets." Tracy jangled the bracelet on her wrist.

"Yeah, that bit is annoying." Juniper edged back toward the table. She had an idea as to how she could try to get out of this.

"I knew Tiffany couldn't resist the lure of gold, so I asked her to come check out the little candy heart in the bathroom." Tracy was practically gloating.

"So that's how it ended up in the drain," Juniper said.

"The drain?" Tracy looked confused. "I actually didn't know where it went. We struggled, and I sort of forgot about it."

"Yep. The police found it in there. That's evidence that you killed Tiffany. And that's not all the police have, so you'd better just turn yourself in now. Hurting me will only get you more time in jail."

"You're lying! The police haven't even been here, so they don't know … and I can't let you tell them. I strangled Tiffany, and now I'll have to strangle you too!"

Tracy lunged at Juniper.

Juniper seized the box of chocolates from the table and hurled them at Tracy. Dozens of them bounced off her onto the floor.

Tracy kept coming toward Juni. Then her left foot smooshed down on a raspberry center, and her right landed on a maple cream filling. She slid across the floor with her legs going in opposite directions, shrieking for dear life, leaving behind a smear of chocolate. Her arms flailed above her head until the back of her skull smashed into the marble countertop, and she tumbled to the ground in a crumpled heap.

Juniper was on top of her in a flash, grabbing the apron and tying it around Tracy's hands to secure them before whipping out her phone and calling the Duckman.

CHAPTER TWENTY

"Good job, Detective Mallard." Stomper leaned against Mallard's office door, his voice gruff, his face in its usual scowl. "At least this one, you solved on your own."

Before Mallard could even thank him, he turned and stomped off down the hall. At least he wasn't in trouble anymore, though it had been a close call this time.

When Juniper had called Desmond to tell him what had happened at Tracy Muller's, he'd actually been on his way over there. He'd suspected Tracy could be the killer, even though Juniper was convinced it was Delilah. Unlike Juniper with her amateur sleuthing,

Desmond used cold, hard facts along with his gut instincts. The facts that pointed to Delilah also pointed to Tracy, so he had wanted to interview her and see what turned up.

He had to admit that Juniper hadn't wanted to beat him to the confession on this one. It had happened by accident, and she also hadn't wanted to stick around to take credit for it. He was actually quite surprised about that. Instead, she'd slunk off before anyone else came, warning Tracy that if she told anyone that Juniper had been there, she would be facing an additional attempted murder charge because Juniper would press charges.

She'd told Desmond that if he needed to say there was another person there, she wanted to remain an anonymous witness if possible. He smiled inwardly. Knowing Juniper, she probably thought she'd solved the case. At least she hadn't rubbed it in.

Sighing, he started back on the amount of paperwork on his desk. A hint of lavender permeated his senses, and he glanced up to see a wispy form barely visible in front of his desk. Tiffany Davenport.

"Thank you, Detective," she said.

"You're welcome," Desmond answered, but by the time he got the words out, she'd already disappeared.

"Did you say something, sir?" Nichols poked his head in.

Desmond smiled. "No. Did you hear something?"

"I thought I did. Must have been my imagination."

"Yes, Nichols. It must have been. Maybe you're working too hard."

Nichols laughed. "Maybe. By the way, nice job on the case, sir."

"Thanks, Nichols." Desmond gave him a genuine smile. "Now, don't you have some filing to do?"

"Yes, sir. I'm off to do that right away, sir."

♥

"I don't know what you did, Juniper," Tori said the next day. "But Stomper has totally gotten off Desmond's case."

Juniper looked up from the Easter egg

hunt clues she was working on and smiled. "Not much, just a little fancy footwork."

After Tracy had slid on the chocolates and knocked herself out, Juniper had called Desmond on his personal phone. He'd rushed over, and once he'd taken charge of the situation, she'd hightailed it out of there before the rest of the police came. Contrary to popular belief, she didn't need to get credit for capturing every killer. She was just glad the whole thing was over with and she could focus on the Easter egg hunt for her next party.

Just then, the scent of lavender filled Juniper's nostrils, and she sneezed.

"You're welcome," Tori said.

"Umm… I think it's supposed to be 'God bless you.'" Juniper itched her nose. That scent was a bit irritating.

"I wasn't talking to you. Tiffany wanted to thank us for helping find her killer."

Juniper's brows rose as a thought occurred to her. "Wait, did you see—"

"Tiffany's ghost? Yeah. Yes, I did."

Juniper swung her head to see if Tiffany was still visible but found the room empty of her presence and Lionel floating there instead.

He cleared his throat.

"Can you see Lionel?" Juniper asked Tori before Lionel could speak.

Tori looked in the bathroom and then shook her head. "No. And, honestly, I'm kind of glad. Seeing Tiffany was... something else."

Juniper would give her that. Looking back to Lionel, she said, "What's up?"

"The young lady wished me to relay her thanks to you all for what you did. She can now rest in peace."

Juniper smiled. "You're welcome, Tiffany," she said, although she had no idea if she could hear her now that she had moved on. Then she turned to Lionel. "Did she say anything else?"

"Yes, mum. She said you have mice." Lionel exited through the wall, leaving Juniper and Tori alone once more.

Juniper and Tori looked at each other and laughed.

"Well, now that that's over, I guess we'd better get going on the plans for Easter." Tori eyed the decorations and notes Juniper had spread all over the room.

Without prompting, Queen's "The Show Must Go On" filled the mansion.

Juniper smiled. "Oh, yes. The show must go on, indeed."

****

MORE BOOKS BY LEIGHANN DOBBS:

Cozy Mysteries

Juniper Holiday Cozy Mysteries
***

Halloween Party Murder
Thanksgiving Dinner Death
Who Slayed The Santas?
Masquerade Party Murder

Mystic Notch
Cat Cozy Mystery Series
* * *

Ghostly Paws
A Spirited Tail

MORE BOOKS BY LEIGHANN DOBBS:

A Mew To A Kill
Paws and Effect
Probable Paws
A Whisker of a Doubt
Wrong Side of the Claw
Claw and Order

Oyster Cove Guesthouse Cat Cozy Mystery Series

***

A Twist in the Tail
A Whisker in the Dark
A Purrfect Alibi

Moorecliff Manor Cat Cozy Mystery Series

***

Dead in the Dining Room
Stabbed in the Solarium
Homicide in the Hydrangeas
Lifeless in the Library

Silver Hollow

MORE BOOKS BY LEIGHANN DOBBS:

Paranormal Cozy Mystery Series
***

A Spell of Trouble (Book 1)
Spell Disaster (Book 2)
Nothing to Croak About (Book 3)
Cry Wolf (Book 4)
Shear Magic (Book 5)

Blackmoore Sisters Cozy Mystery Series
* * *

Dead Wrong
Dead & Buried
Dead Tide
Buried Secrets
Deadly Intentions
A Grave Mistake
Spell Found
Fatal Fortune
Hidden Secrets

Kate Diamond Mystery Adventures
***

MORE BOOKS BY LEIGHANN DOBBS:

Hidden Agemda (Book 1)
Ancient Hiss Story (Book 2)
Heist Society (Book 3)

Mooseamuck Island Cozy Mystery Series
* * *

A Zen For Murder
A Crabby Killer
A Treacherous Treasure

Lexy Baker Cozy Mystery Series
* * *

Lexy Baker Cozy Mystery Series Boxed Set Vol 1 (Books 1-4)

Or buy the books separately:

Killer Cupcakes
Dying For Danish
Murder, Money and Marzipan
3 Bodies and a Biscotti

MORE BOOKS BY LEIGHANN DOBBS:

Brownies, Bodies & Bad Guys
Bake, Battle & Roll
Wedded Blintz
Scones, Skulls & Scams
Ice Cream Murder
Mummified Meringues
Brutal Brulee (Novella)
No Scone Unturned
Cream Puff Killer
Never Say Pie

Lady Katherine Regency Mysteries

***

An Invitation to Murder (Book 1)
The Baffling Burglaries of Bath (Book 2)
Murder at the Ice Ball (Book 3)
A Murderous Affair (Book 4)
Murder on Charles Street (Book 5)

Hazel Martin Historical Mystery Series

***

Murder at Lowry House (book 1)
Murder by Misunderstanding (book 2)

MORE BOOKS BY LEIGHANN DOBBS:

Sam Mason Mysteries (As L. A. Dobbs)
***

Telling Lies (Book 1)
Keeping Secrets (Book 2)
Exposing Truths (Book 3)
Betraying Trust (Book 4)
Killing Dreams (Book 5)

Romantic Comedy
***
Corporate Chaos Series

In Over Her Head (book 1)
Can't Stand the Heat (book 2)
What Goes Around Comes Around (book 3)
Careful What You Wish For (4)

Contemporary Romance
***

Reluctant Romance

MORE BOOKS BY LEIGHANN DOBBS:

Sweet Romance (Written As Annie Dobbs)
Firefly Inn Series
***
Another Chance (Book 1)
Another Wish (Book 2)

Hometown Hearts Series
***
No Getting Over You (Book 1)
A Change of Heart (Book 2)

Sweet Mountain Billionaires
***
Jaded Billionaire (Book 1)
A Billion Reasons Not To Fall In Love (Book 2)

Regency Romance
* * *
Scandals and Spies Series:

MORE BOOKS BY LEIGHANN DOBBS:

Kissing The Enemy
Deceiving the Duke
Tempting the Rival
Charming the Spy
Pursuing the Traitor
Captivating the Captain

ABOUT THE AUTHOR

USA Today best-selling Author, Leighann Dobbs, has had a passion for reading since she was old enough to hold a book, but she didn't put pen to paper until much later in life. After a twenty-year career as a software engineer, with a few side trips into selling antiques and making jewelry, she realized you can't make a living reading books, so she tried her hand at writing them and discovered she had a passion for that, too! She lives in New Hampshire with her husband, Bruce, their trusty Chihuahua mix, Mojo, and beautiful rescue cat, Kitty.

Find out about her latest books by signing up at:
    https://leighanndobbscozymysteries.gr8.com

If you want to receive a text message alert on your cell phone for new releases , text

COZYMYSTERY to (603) 709-2906 (sorry, this only works for US cell phones!)

Connect with Leighann on Facebook:
 https://www.facebook.com/groups/718049055015420

This is a work of fiction.

None of it is real. All names, places, and events are products of the author's imagination. Any resemblance to real names, places, or events are purely coincidental, and should not be construed as being real.

MY FATAL VALENTINE

Copyright © 2022

Leighann Dobbs Publishing

http://www.leighanndobbs.com

All Rights Reserved.

No part of this work may be used or reproduced in any manner, except as allowable under "fair use," without the express written permission of the author.

❦ Created with Vellum